"Shades of Lady Chatterley's Lover," she said with a sigh.

This did feel like an illicit idyll, dangerous and utterly exquisite.

"Except that they were forget-me-nots," Tom said.

"And he didn't weave them into the hair on her head," Lily added.

"Oh, wanton, provocative woman." Tom bent to nibble her earlobe. "Are you daring me?"

She just smiled, luxuriating in the messages of affection and desire emanating from Tom's body—the rays of heat, the darkening eyes, the eagerly parted lips, the hands that seemed unable to have their fill of her.

Without ceremony, he unzipped her jeans and eased them down below her hips...

Jennifer Rose *loves to travel in search of material for her books, but she is happiest in New York City, where she lives with her husband and daughter. If she had more spare time, she would spend it playing backgammon and the Oriental board game go-moku, and growing vegetables on her rooftop.*

Dear Reader:

One of the most exciting things about creating TO HAVE AND TO HOLD has been watching it emerge from the glimmer of an idea, into a firm concept, and finally into a line of books that is attracting an ever-increasing and loyal readership. TO HAVE AND TO HOLD is now nine months old, and that thrilling growth continues every month as we work with more and more talented writers, find brand new story ideas, and receive your thoughts and comments on the books.

More than ever, we are publishing books that offer all the elements you love in a romance—as well as the freshness and the variety you crave. When you finish a TO HAVE AND TO HOLD book, we trust you'll experience the special glow of satisfaction that comes from reading a really good romance with a brand new twist.

And if any of your friends still question whether married love can be as compelling, heartwarming, and just plain fun as courtship, we hope you'll share your latest TO HAVE AND TO HOLD romance with them and dispel their doubts once and for all!

Best wishes for a beautiful summer,

Ellen Edwards

Ellen Edwards
TO HAVE AND TO HOLD
The Berkley Publishing Group
200 Madison Avenue
New York, N.Y. 10016

KISSES SWEETER
THAN WINE
JENNIFER
ROSE

SECOND CHANCE AT LOVE
BOOK

Other books by *Jennifer Rose*

Second Chance at Love
OUT OF A DREAM #4
SHAMROCK SEASON #35
TWILIGHT EMBRACE #86

To Have and to Hold
A TASTE OF HEAVEN #2
KEYS TO THE HEART #11

KISSES SWEETER THAN WINE

Copyright © 1984 by Jennifer Rose

First edition published June 1984

First printing

"Second Chance at Love," the butterfly emblem, and "To Have and to Hold" are trademarks belonging to Jove Publications, Inc.

Printed in the United States of America

To Have and to Hold books are published by
The Berkley Publishing Group
200 Madison Avenue, New York, NY 10016

*For
Deb, Ted,
Sarah, and Aaron*

KISSES SWEETER
THAN WINE

1

LILY LANGDON SURFACED mistily from an unpleasant dream and sought the comforting warmth of Tom's body. Moving cautiously, not wanting to wake him, she inched her way across the cool sheet and spooned herself against the broad expanse of his chest. She resisted the impulse to wiggle her bottom as she nestled in along his legs, trusting that his arms would reflexively encircle her. They did. A small sigh escaped her lips, and she surrendered to the luxurious sensation of total safety.

Emboldened by the soft, steady whisper of Tom's breath in her hair, Lily dared herself to remember the dark dream. She shuddered as it came back to her with the graphic creepiness of a science fiction movie. A mysterious blue rain had fallen, and the vineyards had grown wildly—so wildly that vines had covered the Langdons' big white farmhouse, choking the sunlight off from the windows, strangling the doors, imprisoning Tom and Lily and the children.

Lily forced herself to take deep breaths, to stay inside the dream. She could open her eyes and end it, or rouse Tom from sleep and ask for comfort; but back in New York, in her actress days, she'd learned a better technique for dealing with nightmares. While one part of her went on remembering, submitting to the crazed cruelty of the vines, another part of her floated free and regarded the dream as a stage play she was watching in an empty theater.

"All right, Lily," half of herself directed from her imaginary fourth-row aisle seat. "You have the power to push back those vines. Just turn on all the lights in the house and the rain will dry up. You can do it. You can do anything."

Quickly light conquered darkness. The vines receded to the fields. Lily the director merged with Lily the actress, and both became Lily the dreamer, the sleeper.

Even with its happy resolution, the nightmare hung around Lily's head until early morning. She was relieved to open her eyes to bright sunshine.

Greater relief came from seeing Tom lying next to her. Seven years of marriage had not dulled the sweet shock of shared nights, shared awakenings. The stronger Lily grew, the more she seemed to need the quiet strength that emanated from her husband.

Even asleep, vulnerable as a child, he looked like a rock and a tower to her. Studying his face, she searched for clues to the inner man—as though to understand his strength would be to possess it for herself. At times she almost resented Tom's sureness. Its very existence was an unspoken challenge. He never sought to dominate her, but rather called on her to meet him as an equal. Though he would offer comfort if she asked for it, he preferred to remind her of her own inner resources.

He would have been proud of the way she had handled her bad dream, she thought as she watched a ray of sunlight make a pathway through the growth of beard on his face. But part of her wished she didn't always have to be so sturdy — her own rock and tower.

A smile flickered briefly across Tom's face, tugging at the sensual fullness of his lower lip. Lily wondered enviously what wonderful dream he was having. Unlike her, he never had nightmares. Whatever demons he encountered, he braved — and vanquished — in total consciousness.

His lips moved again, making Lily ache for a kiss. She adored Tom's mouth. It softened the angular planes of his face, hinting at the deep layer of carnality beneath his work-toughened exterior. On a lesser man, that mouth might have looked too hedonistic. But Tom was all muscle and sinew, with a sun-bronzed, tight-fitting skin covering broad shoulders and a pared-down torso. Looking at him awake or asleep, no one could question his determination to be a great winemaker. Nor could anyone doubt that he had nurtured his vineyards with his own sweat.

Sitting up, Lily let her eyes take in the massed black curls with their dusting of silver; the strong, straight nose; the neck that was a little too thick to look comfortable in a buttoned collar and tie. How typically clever of Tom, she thought, to choose a life in rural northern California, where neckties were al-most as scarce as subway trains.

Yes, he was made of heroic stuff, all right—a typically American hero, really, for all his mixed blood and varied influences. Born of an Italian mother and an Irish father, he was as well-versed in English lit-erature as he was in French viniculture. Above all, he was his own man—though he had a great facility for dealing amiably with other, very different, men. He was as respected throughout the Haiku Valley as he was beloved at home.

As Lily sat gazing adoringly, the object of her meditations blinked his olive-green eyes and yawned.

"Hey," he said languorously, reaching for Lily. "What are you doing way up there?" He pulled her unresisting body down and crushed her against him. "I was having the nicest dream about you," he mur-mured into her raven hair. Pushing back the silken strands from the pale Victorian oval of her face, he added, "Shocking, isn't it? Having hot dreams about my lawfully bedded wife?"

"Better than what I dreamed," Lily said. "Rain."

Instantly Tom laid a finger across her lips. "Don't you dare." Their fifty acres of premium wine grapes were ripening gloriously under the steady summer sun. Rain between now and the September crush could produce rot and cause all sorts of other havoc.

Lily contritely kissed the silencing finger. "Sorry, dearest. Maybe it was a lucky dream, like dreaming about breaking a leg the night before a play opens. Come to think of it, that's probably what I *was* dream-ing."

Tom drew Lily into the circle of his arms and pulled

up the sheet and the sampler-pattern quilt for extra coziness. "No jitters, now," he said in the voice that always warned Lily he would brook no weakness. "I'm sure the opening will be a smash. What's more of a natural than *Most Happy Fella* in a real California vineyard setting?"

"I'll tell you what's more of a natural," Lily began daringly, reaching below the bedclothes with lively fingers. After all their shared hours in bed, she knew exactly what to touch, and how, to bring a musical groan of pleasure rippling from Tom's lips.

"You wanton woman. You little witch. That's just what I was dreaming before I woke up. How did you know?" His hands crisscrossed Lily's body, his possessiveness underscored by a casualness of gesture.

Lily smiled mysteriously, inflaming him. He arched over her, pinioning her wrists, teasing her lips with his stubbly chin. Lily retaliated with impudent little flicks of her tongue. Even with the flavor of sleep still upon him, he was pure nectar to her tastebuds.

"To think you once said you weren't a morning person." Tom kissed her eyelids. "Liar."

"Well, I wasn't," Lily said, "until you gave me reason to be." Nibbling on his neck, she sighed happily. Tom had made her a morning, noon, and night person. He had the power to infuriate her at times, but he never put her to sleep.

"Do we have time—?" he began presciently, only to be interrupted by a *rat-a-tat-tat* at their door. Sighs of passion gave way to sighs of resignation.

"Room service," a cheery young female voice called out. "Everyone decent?"

"Married couples are always decent, dear," Lily

said as she and Tom decorously separated and arranged the bedding.

"I'll remember that." Eighteen-year-old Cleo, the picture of farm-girl radiance in her plaid shirt and jeans, entered with a burdened tray.

"What a wonderful surprise," Lily said to her daughter. "Is it our anniversary, and we forgot?"

"Oh, Tibs and I just both happened to be up early, and we know how you are before an opening. Left to your own devices, you wouldn't eat a thing."

"Except neck of husband," Tom whispered suggestively in Lily's ear, his soft breath teasing the nerve-rich orifice.

Cleo gave her mother and step-father a raised-eyebrow look. At once sophisticated and highly sensitive, she sometimes seemed to regard Lily and Tom with detached amusement. Having spent half a lifetime with Lily as a single mother, she was still coming to terms with Lily as a married woman. But Lily knew that Cleo loved Tom wholeheartedly and drew great reassurance from the marriage.

"What's on that tray, my pretty?" Tom asked his step-daughter. Lily thought gratefully that he always knew when to clear the air.

"Coffee, orange juice, and blackberry muffins," Cleo answered pertly, transferring the contents of her tray to a small round table in front of the dormer window. She tossed her long, unbound hair as she completed her task. "Don't get panicky, Tom-Tom. Tibs is on his way up with your bacon and eggs. I don't suppose I could persuade you to eat an omelette, Mother?"

"Sure you could—at lunchtime," Lily said.

"Give me another seven years," Tom put in, "and I'll make a breakfast-eater of her yet, Cleo. As it is, she'll probably eat all the muffins if I turn my back. They smell sensational."

Cleo flushed with pleasure, and Lily once again admired his knack with her. The sensitive side of Cleo demanded constant stroking, and Tom knew just how to dole out the praise without ever being phony. She and Cleo were lucky to have him.

"Thanks, sweet girl," Lily said. "This is quite a treat. Now, if you'll just excuse us for a minute, we'll put on our robes and get to the table before the coffee cools."

"I thought married couples were always decent," Cleo said with a suppressed chuckle, leaving the room and quietly closing the door.

Tom pulled Lily to him. "What's so great about decency, anyway? And what's the hurry about the muffins? I want you for breakfast, lady." His lips teased the full paleness of her breasts, then he let his unshaven chin graze her nipples, an act guaranteed to make her arch her back in desire.

"Eggs!" called a musical baritone from outside the door.

"Who wrote this comedy?" Tom asked with a good-natured grumble as he and Lily once again chastely arranged themselves under sheet and quilt. In a louder voice, he invited Tibs to enter.

"Good morning, star," Lily greeted her twenty-year-old stepson. The lanky, tanned Tibs was set to play Joe, the handsome young troublemaker, in Lily's production of *Most Happy Fella*. "And how did your own breakfast go down?"

"Just fine," Tibs said with a grin. "But will it stay down?" He set his father's bacon and sunny-side eggs on the table.

"Of course it will," Tom boomed. "You're going to be terrific, and you know it."

"That doesn't mean he won't get an attack of nerves," Lily contradicted gently. "Even seasoned pros do. It's nothing to be ashamed of."

Tibs pushed his fingers through his thick, dark hair. Somewhat slighter than his father, he'd inherited his coloring and rich head of hair. He had Tom's purposefulness, too, even if a few lingering adolescent uncertainties sometimes surfaced. Lily counted him as one of her great blessings. Among many other virtues, he gave her a glimpse of the young Tom that she'd been deprived of. Forty now to her thirty-seven, Tom had been thirty-two when they met, and very much fully formed. He laughingly claimed that he'd sprung from the womb with his mind made up about everything, but Lily knew he'd grown and made choices like any other human being. She often wished she'd been present during the creation of the man she so loved.

Tibs left the room, and Lily and Tom wrapped themselves in matching wool-and-cotton plaid robes that had been a Christmas present from their children.

"Well, you did a great job of talking Tibs into being nervous," Tom said with undiluted sarcasm as they sat down at the table.

"Now wait a minute," Lily flared defensively. She took a cooling sip of orange juice. "I just didn't want him thinking he's weak if his stomach tightens up. It's perfectly normal. All that adrenalin being pumped into the system. Every actor experiences it, and some never outgrow it."

"Probably because no one ever encouraged them to outgrow it. Haven't you ever noticed? People take strange delight in each other's weaknesses."

Tom broke a blackberry muffin in two, offering half to Lily. But her stomach was suddenly clenching, and the fragrant bread held no appeal for her.

Of all the days to be at odds with Tom. Swallowing retorts, she tried to think of an amiable way of saying what was on her mind. "You're so understanding with Cleo," she began. "Isn't Tibs entitled to the same consideration? Or does Thomas Olivieri Langdon, Jr., have to be a man of iron, like his father?"

Realizing that she'd been sharper than she'd intended, she held her breath, waiting for Tom to strike back. Instead he grinned and flexed his right bicep in the classic gesture.

"Me man of iron," he said with a grunt. "Son same."

Lily laughed and reached for a muffin. The brief storm between them had dissipated as magically as the rain in her dream, and suddenly she had an appetite. She noted for her internal record that she owed Tom one; he had short-circuited what could easily have escalated into a day-long skirmish. She blanked out the awful memory of some of the fights she and Tom had waged. Sitting here opposite him in their cozy early-New England bedroom, it was easy enough—and infinitely more pleasant—to dwell on what was good and grand in their life.

Consider the children, for beautiful instance. Cleo, her baby, had grown into a vibrant young woman. She loved the natural world and people; and both nature and humankind seemed to return her affection. Lily thought with a brimming heart of how the shy and uncertain Cleo had come to life when Lily and Tom had married, and how Cleo had suddenly had not only a real father and an instant big brother but also all the fertile beauty of Pennyroyal Vineyards. Winemaking was her calling, it seemed. She was working as Tom's apprentice for the summer and had been accepted for the fall term at the prestigious University of California School of Viticulture at Davis.

As for Tibs, Lily knew that no son born of her body could have brought her more joy. Warm, clever, sensitive, he was always ideal company. Since he'd discovered his passion for acting, he and Lily had been closer than ever.

While she was counting her blessings, Lily couldn't leave out the miraculous way in which her work dovetailed with Tom's. At his suggestion, Lily had established the Pennyroyal Theater-in-the-Vineyards. Built onto the tasting room where tourists sampled and bought Tom's vintages, the theater offered a full season of summer stock. For the price of a ticket, theatergoers not only got to see a touring big-name actor or actress along with talented amateur neighbors from the Haiku Valley, but they also got to dine on such delicacies as local salmon and baby lamb, and vegetables from Lily's prize-winning garden. Naturally a Pennyroyal Theater dinner also included the perfect wines.

Last, Lily had to thank the kindly fates for bringing her to Haiku Valley in the heart of Mendocino County. Outside the dormer window she could see the gentle undulations of the hills of northern California—hills that seemed to fold in on themselves, like meringue in a beating bowl, their geometry different from that of any other landscape she knew. In the July sun the hills had been bleached to the pale gold of Rapunzel's hair. Lily had only to walk out behind the white farmhouse to see the promising verdant symmetry of acre upon acre of prime grapes. And underfoot everywhere was wild pennyroyal, with its lovely purple blossoms and its invigorating mint and licorice aroma.

Yet, thanks to a seeming miracle, a mere half hour drive through majestic redwood forests took Lily to a totally different, equally stirring view: the Pacific coast, with its dramatic cliffs rushing down to meet the throbbing blues of the sea. To think that she had once regarded Central Park in New York City as the ultimate in natural beauty!

"Hey, come back," Tom commanded, mopping up egg yolk with a piece of blackberry muffin. "You look as though you're a million miles away."

"Only about twenty miles," Lily said. "I took a quick mental drive up to Little River and Mendocino."

"I hope you remembered to drop off three cases of Chardonnay at Heritage House."

"Sorry, darling. It was strictly a pleasure trip." Lily poured coffee and hot milk into her cup, then sipped the aromatic brew. "So many pleasures this morning," she added.

"Which was more exciting—my body or the café

au lait?" Tom teased. Catching up Lily's right arm, he licked off a dollop of pennyroyal honey that anointed her wrist. "Don't answer. Just tell me what kind of celebration you were planning for after the show tonight."

Lily gazed rapturously into the warm green depths of his eyes. "I'll tell you this much. I wasn't harboring fantasies of café au lait. Oh, Tom—"

The jangling of the telephone cut her off. She padded across the braided oval rug with its mingled shades of green and reached for the disruptive instrument on her side of the simple early-American four-poster bed. Only seven-forty in the morning. Who—?

"Lily? Morning, sweetheart. It's Chris McWhorter here. Didn't wake you, did I?"

He was a New York theatrical agent, and not just any agent—the man who represented Elgin Ives, the lead in *Most Happy Fella.* According to the arrangement, Ives should have boarded a plane for San Francisco ten minutes ago. Lily's heart began to pound as she assured McWhorter she was quite awake. The call could only mean trouble.

"I've got good news and bad news," the agent said, confirming her dread.

"Elgin can't make it, but you got me Luciano Pavarotti?" Lily put a lightness into her voice she didn't remotely feel.

"Close," Chris McWhorter replied. "Elgin can't come—he slipped while he was in the shower this morning, and it looks like a broken collar bone; but I got you a sensational replacement. Hold onto your hat, honey. I got you Mark Davenport."

Lily wasn't wearing a hat, so she sank down onto

the bed and grabbed a post for support. Tom rose from his chair in concern and started toward her.

"Mark Davenport," Lily echoed vapidly, feeling her shoulders tighten. "Subbing for Elgin Ives," she mumbled at Tom as he sat down beside her.

They exchanged looks of very dark amusement— as though an exploding cigar had just gone off in their faces. Mark Davenport was Lily's first husband and Cleo's father.

2

"WOULD YOU LIKE to taste some wine?" Lily asked.

Projecting mightily, she managed to infuse the words with freshness, warmth, and involvement, though she had pitched the question maybe fifty times since she and Tom had opened the tasting room that morning. As self-aware as if there were a mirror in front of her, she curved her full, richly colored lips in a perfect half-moon smile. She deliberately crinkled her eyes in a way that softened her imperious mien and gave her an earthy air.

Her efforts were paying off, she saw at once. The tentative-looking young couple that had just come through the doorway—newlyweds, Lily thought—were grinning eagerly now. Of course they wanted to taste wine; why else would they have come to the Pennyroyal Vineyards tasting room? Now they would very likely buy as well as taste because they would want Lily to be pleased with them.

To be sure, she had to concede, Tom's lovingly blended bottles did a pretty fine job of selling themselves. She hoped the young couple hadn't dulled their palates winery-hopping up and down the Haiku Valley.

"We have four wines available for tasting today," Lily went on. "Chardonnay, Gewurtztraminer, Riesling, and Cabernet Sauvignon." Deciding from their wide eyes that the couple were newcomers to the tasting game, she added, "We recommend that you start with the Chardonnay. It's the driest." She took two stem glasses out of the overhead rack and poured a splash of the pale green-gold Chardonnay into each. "You can almost see those hints of apple and lemon taste in the color, can't you?" she asked confidingly.

Sipping the cool wine, the young husband and wife exchanged glances, then looked back at Lily.

"It has a strong entry," the husband said. He swirled the wine and held it up to the light. "And, um, a lingering finish."

"Nice oak," the wife put in eagerly, pushing her straight blond hair behind her ears. "But not so much oak that it obscures the natural fruit."

Biting back a smile, Lily resisted telling them that she knew exactly which magazine article about California wines they were quoting from. Everyone had to be a beginner at some point, after all. She remembered all too well the banality of her own wine palate—and vocabulary—until Tom had initiated her into real intimacy with the drink of the gods. And, as it happened, the young man and woman were rather accurately describing the wine they were tasting.

Passing behind her to take a bottle of Gewurtztraminer from the cooler, Tom let a strong hand slide lovingly down her hip. "You could sell that pair a case of river water and make them happy," he whispered.

"You're not doing so badly yourself," Lily returned softly, noting that the party of middle-aged bicyclists with whom he was dealing were eagerly reaching for their credit cards and checkbooks.

Really, they'd taken in a small fortune since morning. It was a brilliant, temperate northern California day, with the weather forecasters promising more of the same for the rest of the weekend. Route 128 was filled with a steady stream of traffic.

Pennyroyal Vineyards customarily drew visitors on their way up to Mendocino on the coast, travelers on their way down the coast to San Francisco, and people out for the pure joy of it. The tasting room, built with simple drama out of redwood, was a natural magnet and stopping place, especially with Lily's flamboyant vegetable garden in front. Picnic tables on a screened porch and, of course, the growing fame of the theater enhanced the picture. And Pennyroyal Vineyards wines were becoming more and more prized by the cognoscenti as Tom won gold medal after silver medal at fairs throughout the state.

Glancing at Tom's face as she poured Riesling for her newlyweds, Lily saw the day's success reflected in his deepset, flashing olive-green eyes. The money was only the outward symbol for him. Wine was his art. It was his way of making communion with the world. At times—tense times—Lily had thought of wine as Tom's mistress. Every satisfied customer— even the braggart connoisseurs who thought they knew wine better than he did—added to his strong sense of well-being.

If only Mark Davenport weren't going to invade the exciting, secure world she and Tom had built for themselves and their children!

It wasn't that she harbored resentment against Mark. The failure of the marriage had been as much her fault as his. They'd married on her eighteenth birthday, and she had to admit now that she'd been a very young eighteen, so in love with the theater and so snowed by Mark that she hadn't been able to see straight. At thirty he'd seemed the epitome of sophistication, an actor who'd already graduated from "promising" to "fulfilling his potential."

In any event, she could never hate him or regret the marriage because it had produced Cleo. Mark hadn't been much of a father over the years, but he'd supplied remarkable chromosomes. Lily felt she owed him.

Tom, on the other hand, harbored some anger toward him. Loving Cleo as Tom did, he was at a loss to understand how any man could abdicate his role as her father. Though he admitted to being glad that Mark didn't interfere in her upbringing, he cringed on Cleo's behalf when Mark's birthday presents arrived late and his birthday calls sometimes didn't come at all.

Though Tom had seemed insulted the few times, early in their marriage, when Lily had wondered aloud if he also resented Mark because he had once shared

Lily's bed, she couldn't help wondering if jealousy would rear its ugly head now. Pennyroyal Vineyards was Tom's territory. Seeing Mark on his land, involved with Lily in a theatrical project he had no part of, might provoke all sorts of dormant emotions.

And poor Cleo! How could she escape feeling a tug of loyalties? Tom was the man she seemed to regard as her real father; she'd even chosen to follow in his professional footsteps. Mark was a kind of exotic uncle figure who took her to splashy New York restaurants when she visited him during Christmas vacations. Still, Mark was her biological sire. He probably meant more to her than she was willing to admit to Lily and Tom, maybe more than she was willing to admit even to herself. Would the delicate balance of her feelings for the two men be thrown out of kilter when Mark was here in Tom's corner of the world?

Untypically at a loss for words, Lily hadn't yet told Cleo the news. She'd have to tell her any minute, though. A glance at the clock reminded Lily she'd soon have to leave for Haiku Airport, on the other side of the mountains. Mark's flight from New York would land him in San Francisco at one-fifteen; then, as Chris McWhorter had caustically put it, he would take an Air Haiku "puddle jumper" up to "God's country."

The newlyweds interrupted Lily's musings to ask her if she could ship a case of wine to San Diego. Back in the role of high-powered salesperson, she answered briskly that she could, indeed. Her customers opted for six bottles of Chardonnay, five of the "chewy" red Cabernet Sauvignon, and one bottle of the late-harvest Riesling dessert wine, which the husband said had a "good nose."

The young couple and Tom's bicyclists left with warm good-byes. A mantle of peace—and Tom's left arm—descended on Lily's shoulders in the suddenly silent tasting room. Let New York agents be as sardonic as they liked, Lily thought. This really *was* God's country. Through the wide windows of the tasting room she saw a violet haze of pennyroyal and the shimmering gold of the hills behind the vineyards. Then, for a moment, the darkness of her dream came back to her, and the vines looked almost menacing.

"Tell me everything's going to be all right," she begged Tom.

"Isn't it always?" he said, stroking her hair. "Don't we always muddle through? Mark won't make that much of a difference. He'll probably spend most of his spare time hanging out in his hot tub at the inn or driving up to Mendocino to see the action. And if that agent half spoke the truth, he got good reviews in *Most Happy Fella* in New England last summer, so you'll probably have a big week at the box office. Maybe it'll turn out that Elgin Ives did us a good turn by slipping on his soap."

"That reminds me," Lily said. "I want to call our distributor in New York and have some of our wine sent over to him. What would you want to drink if you had a broken collar bone?"

"Cabernet," Tom said instantly. "Half a bottle on an empty stomach, and he won't need any pain-killers to knock him out."

Lily reached for the phone, but she couldn't quite

let Tom go. "Are we eternal and unshakable?"

A flicker of irritation crossed his face. "What are all these doubts?" he asked, taking Lily by the shoulders. "They upset me. You're Wonder Woman. You shouldn't need so much reassuring."

"I'm Lily, and I do need reassuring, and I want you to do the job," she returned. "We never signed a pact to be reasonable in all our emotional needs, did we?"

"Don't resent your own strength," Tom replied. "Sometimes I think you want to need me more than you really do."

The unmistakable *varoom* of motorcycles blasted the moment apart and drew them hurriedly to the window. They both grinned broadly as they beheld the unlikely sight of two men in clerical collars and plain black suits dismounting from big Harley-Davidsons.

"Just in time to deliver us," Lily said.

"More likely they want us to deliver to them," Tom returned. "How many summer festivals have we made donations to?"

"Oh, well, the credit upstairs can't hurt us," Lily said. In fact, neither she nor Tom had ever turned down a request for a donation to a charitable cause, religious or secular.

Tom put his arms around Lily. "Don't worry about anything," he said, giving her the reassurance she'd been aching for. "Tonight, when we're really alone, I'll show you how eternal and unshakable we are."

"Promise?"

His deep, searing kiss said he promised.

3

LILY SPENT AN extra few minutes in front of her dress-
ing-table mirror perfecting the part in her hair. Dead
center, the part showed off her high Victorian brow
and emphasized her cheekbones. Under Mark's influ-
ence, she'd worn long bangs over her forehead. Tom,
bless him, claimed to delight in her hair as she wore
it now, cut to one length just below her shoulders,
combed slightly off her face, tucked behind her ears,
allowed to hang free.

Was it too young a hairstyle? she wondered briefly,
peering at herself under the theatrical dressing-room-
caliber lights. If there was anything she found grace-
less, it was a woman who imitated her daughters in
fashion. Lily made no attempt to purge her hair of
silver threads, though she admitted to being glad they
didn't grow in greater abundance.

After a long look Lily decided she made the grade. Her hair certainly wasn't matronly; then again, it wasn't girlish either. Cleo, endowed with the same lustrous, naturally wavy jet-color hair, parted it on the side and let it cascade freely—occasionally messily, it seemed to a mother's eye—halfway to her waist. And while Cleo never touched makeup, Lily had no hesitation about making daily use of the cosmetic tricks she'd learned backstage over the years. A thin layer of foundation with a sunscreen in it gave her complexion a finished, silky sheen and protected it from the ravages of ultraviolet rays. A judicious application of cheek and eye color enhanced her features without giving her a painted, city-streets look.

Shortly after her arrival in California, Tom had asked her why she wore "a mask" instead of being natural. "I'm an actress," she'd said. "I have no 'natural.' I feel more myself with makeup on than with my face scrubbed."

Tom had nodded, understanding at once. "I guess I can't complain. I get to see you both ways. And I think you're beautiful both ways."

"I'm not a let-it-all-hang-out person," she'd continued. "You know that, don't you? I'm very controlled, and I have no interest in changing. It makes me feel good to think that strangers see only my mask—that you're the one person who gets to see me naked in every way."

Their conversation had made the delightful progression to literal nakedness, Lily remembered, with strands of "Can This Be Love?" playing in the air.

As Lily relived the moments now, Tom's words and gestures echoing silkily, she felt buoyed by them.

All in all, she and Tom had done a pretty good job of accepting each other over the years. Oh, they'd had their share of misunderstandings and disagreements, but they'd always respected each other's sovereignty. And they shared a common bond that seemed to grow wider and broader and deeper all the time. Sometimes Lily saw them as two different grape varietals grafted onto a single stem.

Then why had she just taken her second shower of the day? Why was she spending so much time applying her mascara in anticipation of a meeting with a man who wasn't Tom?

Meeting her eyes in the mirror, she laughed away the question. Really, it was the most predictable thing in the world for a woman to want to look her best when seeing her ex-husband. She wanted him to know how happy she had been in the last seven years, how much Tom had done for her. She wanted him to know that living in California and being a director—not an actress—suited her to perfection. A face was an advertisement for the soul, especially according to Mark Davenport's values! If he admired the way she looked, he would have to concede that she'd found a level of happiness she never would have known with him.

Still, a pang of guilt persisted. She shouldn't care what Mark thought about her. How would she feel if Margaret, Tom's first wife, were alive and coming to visit—and Tom were primping in front of a mirror? She might understand, but she wouldn't be thrilled. Then again, she reminded herself, she'd never felt hurt by the high regard in which both Tom and Tibs held Margaret Langdon's memory. Margaret had obviously been a sort of saint—loyal, hard-working, and uncomplaining through her long illness. She'd also been a bit colorless, Lily imagined. The sort of woman who followed cookbook recipes exactly and got most of her conversational gambits from her favorite homespun authors. In her most honest heart, Lily thought herself less noble than Margaret, but probably more interesting. They were too different to be in competition.

And so were Tom and Mark, Lily decided emphatically, eager to resolve her internal debate. Tom had generosity of spirit; Mark was obsessed with his own little world. Tom was sure of himself and his place in the universe; Mark had the actor's showy but fragile ego. Above all, Tom knew that he had given Lily and Cleo everything it is within one person's power to give another. Mark could never have that satisfaction, and Tom knew it.

Lily felt a sudden longing for Tom that began as a softening in the spirit and ended as a hard ache in her belly. She mentally telegraphed a fervent message for him to come striding into her dressing room, his eyes dark with hunger. Mistily she shook away the impossible thought. This time of day, when the sun burned hottest, Tom nearly always went out to the fields. While his crew of workers had lunch and took a well-earned rest, he checked the vine leaves for infestation, inspected the irrigation system and fencing, and saw to myriad other details. Business in the tasting room purred along under the capable guidance of Maryanne and Maureen Bailey, twenty-one-year-old twin sisters from nearby Danville.

But *she* could go to Tom! The exciting thought flashed through Lily's mind as she fastened a strand of pearls around her neck. Just as her face seemed more itself with makeup than without, her throat looked distressingly bare unless she wore the pearls Tom had given her on their wedding day. He liked to tease her and say she was going to wear them out, but she knew he was touched that they meant so much to her.

She could go to Tom, out in the fields, before she collected Cleo at the winery and took off for Haiku. And when Mark Davenport stepped off the plane, he would see Thomas Olivieri Langdon, Jr., stamped all over her.

With dizzying speed she pulled on a red silk shirt and a pair of jeans. Washed a hundred times, the jeans were as soft as velvet and fit her as though they'd been custom-made. Hand-tooled cowboy boots of fine wine-red leather completed the outfit. She grabbed a navy and wine leather pouch, slung it over her shoulder, and hurried downstairs.

Dorothy White, a thin, gray-haired widow from Danville who helped out with the house, was vacuuming the living room carpet. She turned off the noisy machine and looked inquiringly at Lily.

"See you later, Mrs. White," Lily said breathlessly. "I'll be back around four. Be sure to try one of the muffins Cleo made."

Before her housekeeper could do more than nod, Lily had dashed out the back door, across the redwood terrace, and down to the old barn that served as a garage. She noted with satisfaction that the Jeep was in its usual place and the tractor at rest, as well. Tom hadn't gone out to the farthest vineyards, as she'd feared. Thinking back over their conversation at breakfast, she remembered he'd mentioned something about the new Gamay Beaujolais plantings. She started walking briskly in the direction of the irrigation pond and the new plantings.

The vista in all directions was so shining that she almost forgot her goal. Tom's meticulously spaced vines, each bound to a slender stake, formed a beautiful grid of straight lines that appealed on some primal level to Lily's love of order and control. At the same time, the folded hills with their golden grasses dancing in the wind called to her need for freedom and mischief.

Between the green of the grapes and the blue of the pond, she caught a glimpse of red. Her heart beat faster. Tom was wearing a red and white checked shirt.

Her mind beat faster, too. How on earth was she going to explain her presence out here? Inexplicable shyness tempered the heat of her blood. Tom was her husband and her lover, and he'd invited her to share the delights of bed later that evening; but something held her back from plainly declaring her lust out in the sun-drenched fields.

Silly excuses flew through her mind. She could tell Tom she couldn't find the keys to the Datsun, though they were no doubt in the ignition. She could tell him his sister had called from Los Angeles—true enough, but hardly the sort of exciting news that merited a breathless trip to the fields. She could—

"Lily!"

He had seen her and was coming to meet her, his face split by a smile, his arms wide open.

"You heard me!" he said, pressing his lips to hers, inhaling the clean fragrance of her hair.

"Heard you?"

"Thinking about you. Lustful thoughts unbecoming to a middle-aged married man." He stepped back to take a better look at her. "You're one gorgeous woman, you know that?" Looking down at his dusty jeans, he added ruefully, "Too gorgeous to touch."

"Too hungry not to touch," Lily murmured, all vestiges of shyness gone. Tom was her husband and her lover, and he wanted her as much as she wanted him.

The sun beat down on them, its awesome power offset by the cooling breeze that ricocheted off the hills. From the farm that bordered their land came the muted *baa-baa* of sheep. The sweet spice of pennyroyal filled Lily's nostrils. She felt suffused with sensations of the natural world. It was as if the longing in her limbs and the smoldering glint in Tom's eyes were one with the rhythms of the earth.

Tom pulled off his work gloves and flung them to the ground. Silently he reached out his strong fingers and stroked Lily's throat, feeling the surge of her pulses.

She opened her mouth to speak, but no sound emerged.

"I know," he said softly. "I know." His hands moved upward into the dark silk of her hair, and he pulled her toward him. His lips pressed hers gently at first, then with a savage heat that made her think her knees would surely give way. Had she truly woken up next to him, shared morning coffee and family chit-chat with him, this sun-bronzed god of the grapes? Were her exquisite tremors of abandonment really for the man whose flesh was lawfully one with her own?

His hands were everywhere, caressing her back, swirling over her buttocks and hips, moving boldly up the front of her shirt to capture the silken hills of her breasts. Deftly he unbuttoned her shirt, leaving only the gossamer lace of her bra between her most sensitive skin and the sensual mix of sun and breeze.

"I want you, Mrs. Langdon," Tom said, his voice low with urgency.

The breeze grew stronger, making his dark curls dance in the sunlight, fanning the flames of Lily's desire. Suddenly it didn't matter why she had come out to the field or who would see her later. Tom was all that mattered, Tom and her own insistent pulses and the symphony of love in her heart.

"Dearest," she murmured, as he urged her down onto the soft carpet of pennyroyal.

"I love you. I love you so much. Love you and want you crazily much." Tom deftly removed her red silk shirt and bra, a hum of appreciation coming from him as Lily's nipples sprang to life, grateful for freedom and his attention. First his fingers, then his lips paid homage to the tingling flesh. "You have the breasts of a seventeen-year-old," he whispered. "The skin of a seventeen-year-old, even in this light. Your body is the world's most beautiful liar."

"Does that mean my breasts are too small?" Lily's tongue underscored the words as she mouthed them into his ear.

"Lord, woman, how many years are we going to have to be married before you believe I think your breasts are perfect? That all of you is? But I guess if I can feel as though this is the first time, you can too."

"Always the first time," Lily said thickly, her speech sounding almost drunken to her ears. "Always." She began unbuttoning his shirt, eagerly reaching for the soft mat of black and silver hair, pulling him on top of her so her breasts could share the sensation with her fingers. Time and the world seemed to vanish as the earth cradled her and helped her to sustain her glorious burden.

Tom's heated lips pressed against hers. She stared with immeasurable delight into the warm green-brown pools of his eyes until the sheer fire of his probing tongue forced her to close her own eyes. She opened them again as she felt Tom spreading her hair across the ground. Laughing tenderly, he snapped a stalk of pennyroyal off at its base, sending a cloud of fragrance into the air, and wove it into her hair.

"Shades of *Lady Chatterley's Lover*." She sighed. This did feel like an illicit idyll, dangerous and utterly exquisite.

"Except that they were forget-me-nots," Tom said.

"And he didn't weave them into the hair on her head," Lily added.

"Oh, wanton, provocative woman." Tom bent to nibble her earlobe. "Are you daring me?"

She just smiled, luxuriating in the messages of affection and desire emanating from Tom's body— the rays of heat, the darkening eyes, the eagerly parted lips, the hands that seemed unable to have their fill of her.

Without ceremony, he unzipped her jeans and eased them down below her hips. Pausing briefly to admire the subtle magic of ivory lace bikini panties against ivory skin, he gently pulled down the panties, too.

Not quite dressed and not quite undressed, lying alone with her husband in the scant shadow of the vineyards, Lily felt exposed and vulnerable. All control seemed to be slipping away from her; yet she wasn't uneasy. Tom was there, not just strong in his own right but strong for her. And he was breaking off another pennyroyal stalk, tickling her belly with its fuzzy purple blossom, doing his mischievous weaving...

A sudden storm of passion overtook them both. As Tom undid his work boots and jeans, Lily twisted out of hers.

Seeing Tom's readiness for her, feeling sun and wind on her most intimate flesh, Lily writhed with passion and called out for her lover to take her. Teasing her at first, entering her with a deliciously torturous slowness, Tom suddenly had to give way to the momentum of his feeling. He edged his hands between Lily and the fragrant earth and pulled her toward him as he took her with a thrusting urgency. Then, as though conspiring to prolong their shared ecstacy, both bodies slowed almost to stillness. Scarcely moving, scarcely breathing, they slid into the nameless place where every notion is like a poem, every movement is like a ballet.

I want to live here, Lily thought, certain that Tom's mind was piping a similar message. She felt utterly lost in her man, yet ultimately found. Then mind and body ceased to be separate, and thought and feeling became one. A sweet fire was consuming her, consuming them both, burning away all barriers. Truly one flesh, they subsided into each other's arms.

"Lily. Dearest," Tom murmured gently when he could speak. "Most wondrous of women."

"No, it's you," was all she could say, sinking into him, longing to slide off into a dream from which she would never awaken.

Tom brought her back to this world by reminding her that she had to collect Cleo and drive to Haiku to meet Mark's plane. The purpose for her trip out to the fields had been swept from her mind by the power of her longing and the peace that followed it. Inwardly blushing, she knew she should feel guilty because something besides pure passion had initially sent her in search of Tom.

"Do you want to use the washhouse?" he asked. He'd built a sanitary facility near the irrigation pond for his field workers. "Not that I'd mind if Mark knew how you spent the last half hour."

Lily laughed in relief. Her thoughts hadn't been venal, after all—merely human. No one could possibly question the genuineness of her hunger for Tom, this afternoon or any other time.

"Mark is one thing and Cleo's another," she said. "I definitely want a wash. Will you ride shotgun?"

Trading tender glances, they dressed, then started toward the pond arm in arm, singing softly as they went.

4

THE DRIVE FROM Pennyroyal Vineyards to the city of Haiku involved a series of hairpin turns on the lip of plummeting cliffs. After seven years of making the journey once or twice a week, Lily still held her breath behind the wheel. She was grateful for the heft of the dark-green Datsun, with its low center of gravity, and for the scarcity of other traffic. But she wouldn't really relax until they were over the mountains.

Cleo, in the passenger seat, softly hummed folk tunes under her breath. She understood how her mother felt about the drive and tactfully refrained from distracting conversation. Lily was doubly appreciative of Cleo's discretion today. Though she knew she looked as pristine and polished as ever, and gave off a faint, unrevealing aroma of rose-and-vanilla dusting powder, she felt sexual vibrations bouncing off her body.

Cleo would never pry into Lily and Tom's private life, but Lily still feared the innocent question that might produce a blush on her part. Silence was, all in all, welcome.

Staying as close to the center line as she could, Lily negotiated the torturous double turn known locally as the Dromedary's Humps. To her left, the mountain jutted into the road with an oppressive intensity. To her right, the road dropped away into sheer nothingness, with only a flimsy guardrail between the car and black eternity.

To think that Tom actually regarded this drive as fun! Even coming home at night from a wine-tasting in Haiku, he easily slipped into the rhythms of the curves. She actually had known him to sing a little ditty about the Dromedary's Humps, as if the road were some kind of beloved pet.

Lily let out a whooshing sigh of relief as she emerged onto a straightaway. There was still that yawning drop to the right, but at least the hairpin turns were done with. On the ride back home from Haiku, there would be the relative bliss of hugging the mountain rather than the edge of the cliff.

"Well, that's the worst of it," she said. "You all right, baby? Nobody should have to put up with me on these trips."

"Tom says another seven years and you'll be used to the drive," Cleo returned indulgently.

"That's what he says about everything." Lily's hands tightened on the wheel as an old Chevrolet rattled past her from the other direction, then she relaxed again. "I'd sooner hold out hopes for someone building a more sensible road in the next seven years."

"I'm sure Tom would move the mountains for you if he could."

Cleo's voice sounded wistful to her mother's ears, and Lily briefly took a hand off the wheel to pat her daughter's knee. "What a lovely thing to say. He'd move mountains for you, too, sweetie."

"Oh, it's not the same. I mean, I adore getting all that daddy love from him, but I wish . . ." Her voice trailed off, and Lily felt her staring out into the mountainous void. "Well, I wish some man felt that way about me. As a woman, I mean, not just a daughter."

Lily caught her breath. It seemed only moments —seconds—ago that Cleo had been a young girl, with a mouthful of braces and a mind full of uncertainties about boys. Now here she was, construing herself as a woman, casting a longing eye on the world of men.

"You're a wonderful and a beautiful young woman," Lily said, choosing her words with care. "You deserve the love of a wonderful man, and there's no doubt in the world that you'll have it. But there's no rush. You have college to think about, and your winemaking."

"You were only my age when you met Daddy." Cleo's voice had gone higher, and Lily feared that tears were coming.

"Yes," Lily said gently, "and look at what a botch I made of things. I've never stopped being glad that I married him, because the marriage produced you; but no one can accuse me of having used great judgment back then as to who should be the man of my life."

Cleo was silent, and Lily found herself hoping the conversation had just gone away. Ordinarily she longed

for intimate chat with the sometimes-reticent Cleo—
but not on a day when she had to contend with the
Dromedary's Humps, a visit from her ex-husband,
and a show opening!

But Cleo seemed determined to carry on. "Would
you have fallen in love with Tom and married him if
you'd met him when you were eighteen?"

Lily eased around a curve. Thinking she heard traffic
behind her, she checked her rearview mirror but found
only a comforting emptiness. "I don't know," she
answered honestly. "I like to think so, but maybe he
would have intimidated me. I was doing so much
groping myself, I'm not sure I could have stood to be
around someone who'd figured out all his own answers. And I'm not at all sure he would have liked
me." As a memory from the idyll in the vineyards
sneaked up on her, she doubted her own words. Hadn't
their bodies been fashioned for each other? Wouldn't
they have felt some inescapable urge toward each
other those many years ago, even if the rational parts
of themselves had argued against the union?

"Sweetie," she went on, "you know how much I
love talking about these things with you. But right
now my mind is so full of silly details. What do you
say we go out to lunch tomorrow and take up where
we left off?"

There was silence, then Cleo said, "Okay."

Sensing a certain heaviness between them, Lily
quickly moved to change the mood. "Are you looking
forward to seeing your father perform?"

"I sure am," Cleo said eagerly. "The last time I
saw him on a stage was in that awful off-Broadway

musical you and Tom took me to see. Before you were married and everything. What was it called?"

"No Tern Unstoned," Lily reminisced, chuckling. "Yes, we had some notion that it was important for the three of us to see your father on stage. We didn't know it was going to be a play about a man who tries to get birds to smoke marijuana! It's a good thing Tibs was back in California. That might have sworn him off the stage forever."

Mother and daughter shared a companionable laugh, and for a blissful few moments Lily found herself actually enjoying the perilous road. She felt Cleo's mood change to one of restless eagerness, perhaps signaling that the girl was excited and a little bit nervous, too, about seeing her father. Miraculously, she and Cleo were on time, so she didn't have to compound her driving jitters by leaning on the accelerator.

"What's so nice about this surprise visit of Mark's," Lily said, "is that you'll not only get to see him work, but also that he'll get to see you work."

"Oh, Mom, do you think he'll care?" Cleo burst out, as though the question had been welling up in her. "He's such a city person. I'm sure it never occurred to him to connect vineyards and wine. Actually, I don't think he cares much about wine at all. I remember the last time I visited him and we were having dinner at one of those steak houses he loves; he sipped Scotch through the whole meal, and he made fun of some people at the next table who were carrying on about a 1959 Burgundy—a Nuits-St. Georges, I think it was."

"You're just like Tom," Lily said affectionately.

"He can forget everything I said over a dinner and what we both ate, but he'll remember what wine the strangers at the next table were drinking. Cleo," she went on, "you know how much Tom cares about you, don't you? I want you to enjoy your father's visit here—and Tom wants that, too, I know—but you won't let Tom feel left out, will you?"

"Is that what Tom thinks might happen?" Cleo asked incredulously. Instantly she answered herself, "Of course not. He's much too sure of himself. That's *you* worrying, Mother, isn't it? Are you worried that you're the one who's going to make Tom feel left out when you and Mark get all involved in your production?" As if feeling her mother bridle, she went on, "Okay, okay, I know it's none of my business, but please don't lay your hang-ups on me."

Lily watched, stricken, as Cleo blew her nose into a tissue and wiped her eyes. Cleo was so smart, so good, so dear. If only she weren't as sensitive as a sore tooth!

"Honey, I didn't mean to hurt your feelings. Of course Tom trusts you, and I do, too. But I don't think it's fair of you to suggest that I'm projecting. It's just that I think the business of juggling two fathers is a pretty tricky one. Somehow I thought it would be easier for you if you were aware of that. Believe me, I think you've been a wonderful daughter to both men, and I know that's what you'll go on being. You okay, darling?"

"Sure," Cleo said, rubbing her eyes with her fists like a small child. "I'm sorry if I snapped, Mother. But I wasn't way off base, was I? I mean, won't it be tricky juggling two husbands?"

Lily brought the car to a stop at the Route 101 intersection. "It's different," she said, waiting for the signal to change. "Mark is my ex-husband. And there's really no such thing as an ex-father."

"I guess not," Cleo said. But even as she spoke, Lily wondered how true her own glib words actually were.

Her mind raced back through time as she tried to sort out her feelings. If she hadn't gotten pregnant with Cleo, she and Mark probably would have separated even earlier in their marriage than they had. Would they have remained friends if they didn't share a child? she wondered.

She thought of other divorced couples she'd known in New York. Some of them seemed to have a better relationship after the split than before. Vivid pictures flickered through her mind of ex-spouses embracing fondly at parties, consulting each other about new romances, sometimes even rekindling the old spark and becoming lovers again.

She just couldn't envision Mark and herself as part of that pattern. If it weren't for Cleo, she doubted they'd still have each other's addresses.

What an irony, really. Mark had been upset by Lily's pregnancy, coming as it did when they were quarreling more often than not and were also beset by money worries. Only the dim hope that the new baby might magically bring them together—and a feeling that a child deserved two parents—kept them together during those trying months.

When Cleo had arrived, Mark had found her more a nuisance than a delight. He and Lily had both quickly realized that a clean break would probably be better for the baby than the dubious pleasure of living with two bickering parents, one of whom resented her existence.

Though Lily had delighted in being a single mother, as if Cleo were a beautiful doll she didn't have to share, she knew that Cleo would someday need to know her father. And she never lost hope that Mark would someday grow into fatherhood. Without being oppressive or trying to make him feel guilty about his lack of paternal feelings, she'd kept Cleo on his mind after the divorce. She'd sent him snapshots, crayon drawings, copies of Cleo's first poems. Meanwhile, she made Mark a real and lovable figure for Cleo. She'd always encouraged the child to think that her father cared for her, even if he didn't show his affection in the usual ways.

Lily's work had paid off. When Cleo was nine, Mark was forty—and starting to feel mortal. Suddenly he'd been ecstatic that he had a child, a link with the future, though brief visits with her seemed to satisfy him. He'd even expressed regret over the divorce, especially after Tom came into Lily and Cleo's life, and Mark saw a new family forming.

Lily might tell herself that Tom was her only husband, really her first true husband. But Mark was still the man who had fathered Cleo. He wasn't totally "ex." Maybe there was no such thing as someone who was totally "ex." What was it her sister, Dorrie, used to say? "If it didn't last, it wasn't love." But it had been love, hadn't it? Not mature love, to be sure, but not something trivial, either.

Instantly she rejected the idea that she had loved Mark. It seemed too disloyal to Tom. What she felt for Tom, and only Tom, was love—the one kind of love worthy of the name. Or was it?

As if to dispel the disturbing thoughts, she slipped back into the swirling memory of her wild tango with Tom in the vineyards. She forgot about such mundane matters as traffic lights as her skin relived his ardent touch. Mark might still have some claim on her soul, but only Tom Langdon spoke the language of her body.

At Lily's side, Cleo gave a giggle. "Hey, they passed a new law, Mom. It's legal to go on green in California."

"Is it?" Lily returned brightly, making a hasty left turn onto Route 101 and heading toward the airport. "I must remember that."

A zigzag through the shopping district took them to Haiku Airport. With its corrugated-tin terminal and generally unprepossessing look, the small field was a far cry from the glamour of air travel as suggested in TV commercials. But it had an impressive safety record and was the home base for an intrepid helicopter crew known for rescue work in the mountains.

"There he is!" Cleo cried, pointing to a tall, slim man in a dark suit with a trench coat over his arm.

Lily said nothing, afraid that her suddenly hammering heart would betray her. Cleo had decided at age fourteen that she was perfectly capable of flying across the country alone for her annual visits with her father, so Lily hadn't seen him in nearly five years. It threw her to see how attractive he was at forty-nine. He wasn't a conventionally handsome man, but his hooded eyes and twice-broken nose made his face arresting and oddly appealing. He was the sort of actor a casting director would immediately envision as the devil in dinner clothes or one of those ultimately lovable Brechtian underworld figures. It was going to take a lot of padding around his middle to turn him into Tony in *Most Happy Fella*, not to mention a wig to suggest baldness.

Lily hung back as Cleo and Mark embraced. Her thoughts were whirling again. Should she offer him her hand to shake, or her cheek to kiss? One seemed too formal, the other too intimate.

Mark solved the problem by grabbing Lily in a G-rated bear hug, then holding her at arm's length to get a better look at her.

"It's a good thing you take after your mother in the beauty department," he said to Cleo in his gravelly after-hours voice. "The woman positively refuses to age. Lily, you look as young and gorgeous as you did the day I met you."

"And you're as full of blarney as you were that day," Lily returned, trying to deny herself the pleasure of feeling flattered by his words. She was strangely relieved to note that Mark's mahogany hair, expensively cut just above collar length, showed signs of having been tinted. All things were revealed under the California sun!

"Do you have luggage we should be seeing about, or did you just travel with your usual bagful of corny jokes and glib remarks?"

"You can take the girl out of New York, but you can't take New York out of the girl," Mark said, grinning. "Come to think of it, I do have luggage. I couldn't visit you in this wilderness without bringing you a few trinkets from civilization, could I?"

"Oh, Dad," Cleo said indulgently, as if his banter was familiar and tolerable to her. But Lily felt genuinely affronted. She retaliated inwardly by taking very close stock of Mark and deciding, with grim satisfaction, that "civilization" had taken its toll on him. Under his thick, expressive eyebrows, his pale-blue eyes looked definitely bloodshot. And his slimness somehow spoke of health clubs and bizarre diets— in contrast with Tom's naturally honed and fit body.

She reminded herself that the man had just stepped off a two-pronged plane trip; a little charity was in order. But he hardly looked as though he wanted charity. Mark Davenport obviously thought exceedingly well of himself, in every aspect. If Tom exuded a kind of quiet self-confidence, Mark gave off hot sparks of a noisy self-love.

"What is this Haiku business, anyway?" Mark asked, as they claimed his two heavy leather bags from an old baggage cart that was the antithesis of modern airport automation. "I thought a haiku was a Japanese poem."

"It is, but it's also a native American word meaning 'beware the New York actor,'" Lily shot back. Then, regretting the way she kept slipping into Mark's style of repartee, she added, "It's really very lovely country out here, Mark. Wait till you see the redwoods. Wait till you see our place."

As they reached the Datsun, Lily couldn't help saying, "Look, Mark, I didn't lock it. When's the last time you saw an unlocked car in New York?"

"I've got to hand it to you, kid," he rumbled as he stowed his bags in the trunk. "Of course, in New York you don't need to get into a car every time you want a quart of milk or a newspaper. How far do you have to drive to get *The New York Times?*"

"This may come as a surprise, Mark, but the world out here doesn't revolve around what the *Times* says. Though, as it happens, we get the Sunday *Times* in Mendocino every week. Where we also get better croissants than I ever ate in Manhattan."

As though eager to get out from between her sparring parents, Cleo ducked into the back seat of the Datsun. For an instant Lily felt betrayed, but then she had to concede that Mark's long legs were hardly suited to the sportscarlike dimensions of the 280 ZX rear quarters.

"Well, old girl," he began jovially, as Lily turned onto the road toward home, "here we are again. Did we ever figure on California?"

"Never," she said lightly, trying to cover the anxiety he aroused in her by making his presence in her car sound like a collaborative adventure.

"Remember how we used to make fun of all those 'laid back' folks out here?" he persisted. "All those down-to-earth, back-to-the-soil folk?"

"Like me, you mean?" Cleo piped up from the back, causing her mother to heap silent blessings on her head.

"Me, too," Lily was emboldened to say. "Cleo's the one who communes with the vines, but I have what just happens to be one of the better-looking vegetable gardens around."

"Veggies!" Mark chortled. He took a long sideways glance at Lily, as if trying to make sure he hadn't inadvertently accepted a ride with a stranger. "I remember the days when you thought the only vegetable worth eating was a side order of fried onions with your steak."

Had there really been such a time? Lily wondered in a panic. She did remember how startled she'd been the first time Tom suggested they have a salad for dinner. Even a salad at lunchtime had been her idea of fare for dieters, a group she'd never had to be part of. How surprised and relieved she'd been when Tom's salad had turned out to be a delicious and satisfying cornucopia of ingredients, not the rabbity offering of leaves she'd expected.

"People do change," Lily said. She was on the mountain road now, too focused on driving to watch her words. "You've changed."

"Have I?" Mark pounced. "Tell me all about it."

As Lily shifted down to take a curve, her hand grazed his leg. Stung, she managed to grind the gears. "You've got mahogony hair," she said in retribution, though part of her wanted to acknowledge that Mark had gotten more attractive with the passing of time. "You dress like a grown-up now," she added as a kind of compromise.

"I've always dressed like a grown-up," Mark returned. "It wasn't so noticeable to you when you dressed like one, too. Though I like the pearls, kid. You miss New York?" he asked, not skipping a beat. "I can't really believe that bean sprouts mean more to you than bright lights. Lord, what a kick I used to get out of watching your face when we walked around Times Square. If you were ever feeling blue, the lights would bring you right up. Remember?"

"I remember," Lily said softly, moved in spite of herself. "But wait until you see the moon and stars out here. No Broadway billboard can compete with that light show."

"I saw it all at the Planetarium," Mark said dismissively. "Amateur stuff."

"Oh, Dad," Cleo said, in her good-humored way. "You're such a character."

"I am, am I?" Mark said easily, turning to look at his daughter. "Well, I suppose there are worse ways of being perceived by one's progeny. You serious about this wine stuff, Cleo? You know, it's just a passing fad. Like bean sprouts. Believe me, a couple of years and America will rediscover whiskey. Any hostess who tries throwing a wine and cheese party will be out."

"You don't really understand wine, Dad," Cleo said, her voice more tremulous than jaunty now. "You think one kind of scotch is a world away from another kind but that all wines are the same."

"They are when it comes to the headache department," Mark returned.

"There are histamines in red wine that do sometimes bring on headaches in people who are migraine-prone," Cleo said importantly, "but white wine is much more innocuous. And, of course, a well-made wine—"

"Water," Mark said. "That's what I think of white wine. Designer water."

Lily and Cleo had to laugh.

"Come on, Dad," Cleo said. "Wait until you taste our Chardonnay. It's really a mouth-filling wine. You'll see."

"I still wish you were leaving yourself open to more choices in the future," Mark said, his voice serious now. "Getting a liberal arts education instead of narrow training."

"I'll be studying liberal arts, too," Cleo said. "I want to be really good in French, so I can maybe work in Burgundy or Bordeaux for a while—that's what a guy from the Valley is doing, Gideon Alexander. And when you hear Shakespeare and T. S. Eliot and D. H. Lawrence quoted at the dinner table," she added spiritedly, "it makes you grow up pretty interested in books. I'll be taking lit courses, too."

"Mmm," Mark said, sounding less than convinced but obviously not wanting to press the conversation to the point of unpleasantness.

At the mention of D. H. Lawrence, Lily felt heat rise in her body as she remembered Tom and his sensual games with pennyroyal. Eager to distract her passengers as well as herself, she said to Mark, "I hope you'll like your accommodations. The Haiku River Inn isn't exactly the Plaza, but it's very comfortable."

"Sounds like a Zen retreat." Mark sniffed. "Do I have to eat—what do you call that bean curd stuff—tofu for breakfast? What about that place where the Neil Simon movie was shot? Isn't it around here?"

"Heritage House? Booked way in advance, and about four times the cost of the inn," Lily snapped. "And about twenty minutes farther away. Since I know you hold that only peasants have driving licenses, I thought you wouldn't mind making it a little easier on those of us who are going to be chauffeuring you every time you want some special kind of East Coast tissue to blow your beautiful nose in."

"Well, excuse me," Mark said, amusement in his

voice. He made a point of staring out the window at the awesome scenery of the Dromedary's Humps, humming melodies from *Most Happy Fella* under his breath. Then the humming stopped, and silence reigned.

Lily knew she'd overreacted. Really, though, he'd gone just a bit far in insulting all things Californian. The worst part was that he was too clever a man to believe everything he'd said. Surely he knew that wine was ancient and eternal, anything but a passing fad. Granted, there had been a recent plague of amateur oenophiles boring everyone to death with their rhapsodies, but that didn't change the true status of wine. Mark very obviously had been indulging in that favorite New York pastime, putting people down. She remembered his frequent comments to the effect that it was worth a few tears (someone else's, of course) to get off a good line.

How different Tom was, how wonderfully different! Mark probably considered Tom's style devastatingly boring, for it wasn't really a style at all. He said things because he believed them. Lily might cavil at his macho ways, but she could never accuse him of putting them on. Sometimes, she had to admit, she wished she were up against ideas less deeply cherished. But ultimately how much more satisfying and safe to share a life with someone whose words were backed by ideas and credos! Mark was all too apt to change his personal party line from day to day just to allow some witty turn of phrase to come into the world.

As she drove past the tasting room on the way to the Haiku River Inn, Lily gently beeped the horn in her special signal to Tom. It seemed forever and a year since they'd lain in each other's arms, blissfully forgetful of the world. Why did some dark voice inside her persist in saying it would be forever and a year before they shared such a brilliant passage again?

She called on all her actress's discipline and made herself think of other things. The play might flop that night, and the cold poached salmon at the dinner theater might be overcooked and mushy. She surprised herself by chuckling softly at the idea. In comparison with her morbid thoughts about some terrible schism with Tom, failure all around at the theater was an almost pleasant prospect.

"Here we are," she said in a burst of gaiety as they approached the Haiku River Inn.

"Swell." Mark grunted, eyeing the collection of cabins and shingle-front main house. "Which one of those outhouses is mine?"

Her voice stiff again, Lily said, "I booked you a private cabin because each one has a hot tub. If you'd rather stay in the lodge, I'm sure they can accommodate you."

"Lodge? Do I look like an Elk?" Mark gazed dismally out the window. "Where's the bar?"

"There's a sit-down bar in the main house," Lily said, "along with what I think is one of the best dining rooms in the region. I also asked to have a bottle of Chivas Regal and a supply of mineral water put in your cabin. Do you think you'll survive?"

Mark patted her on the shoulder, his fingers lingering an instant. "So you haven't forgotten everything I taught you, after all." Seeming to realize that some greater effort at civility was required of him, he let his head bobble up and down in a series of approving little nods as he took a fresh look at the landscape in front of him. "Is that a redwood tree?" he asked, pointing.

"It's a telephone pole," Lily said.

With a minimum of speech, she got Mark registered, arranged to pick him up for a rehearsal after he'd had time to shower and unwind, and headed for the sanity of home.

 5

TOM ALWAYS SAID his Italian blood spawned his love
and knowledge of grapes but his Irish blood set the
pace of his day. He liked tea at five o'clock, and
today—as on most days—Lily joined him in their
big white kitchen for a pot of Barry's Best and nutty-
tasting wholemeal soda bread. The tea was shipped
twice a year from a grocer in County Cork, who also
supplied the bread flour. Sweet butter and bitter-
orange marmalade rounded out the repast.

Though the ritual was Tom's, Lily now found it
an important part of her daily life. For one thing, the
kitchen always provided her with a measure of contentment, no matter how demanding and frenzied the
rest of the day had already been. With its exposed
redwood beams providing a warm look and gleaming
white walls adding a note of coolness, the room echoed

the balanced blend of hot sun and zesty breezes that made Haiku Valley summers so delicious. The copper and stainless-steel cookware hanging from crossbeams invited experimentation but didn't reproach the chief cook on days when she was too busy to do more than hand Mrs. White a menu. The early-American master bedroom upstairs provoked a stark intimacy that Lily needed and loved; the kitchen did something at least as important—it let her just hang out.

Lily smiled happily as Tom came in through the outside door, smelling of sun and earth. She moved into kissing range so that she could taste the day's work on him before he scrubbed his face and hands at the big metal sink.

"Is there no satisfying you?" he teased as her lips hung around his mouth, obviously hungry for a second kiss. "I hope not," he answered his own question, giving her what she wanted.

She brought the kettle up to the boil and rinsed out the teapot with scalding water as Tom rolled up his sleeves and began to scrub.

"Everything go all right with Mark?" he asked.

"I think so. We had a good run-through. I liked his chemistry with Missy Clarkson."

Tom grunted something under his breath, something derogatory-sounding.

"He is a fine actor," Lily said defensively. She spooned tea leaves into the warmed pot and poured in boiling water. Giving the tea a swift stir, she put the lid on the pot, covered it with a knit cozy, and set the pot on the table.

"Didn't say he wasn't."

Lily sighed deeply. This wasn't the relaxed, jaunty lover she'd left a few hours earlier. Had he spent the intervening time brooding about her reunion with Mark?

"Tom?" she began tentatively. "Do you mind awfully? About Mark's being here?"

Wiping his forearms with paper towels, Tom turned from the sink. "I don't mind at all. Why should I mind? I'm glad that agent was able to find a replacement for Ives on such short notice. You've got enough to worry about as it is."

They sat down opposite each other, and Lily splashed milk into each of their teacups as Tom began slicing thick rounds of bread.

"I thought I didn't have a worry in the world," she said lightly. "Unless someone saw us out there in the field today?"

Tom smiled thinly. "I didn't get any winks and guffaws from the men, if that's what you mean."

Lily scraped butter across a piece of bread. She was dying to understand Tom's mood, but she knew him; he didn't take well to probing. This man who was capable of the deepest intimacy also had a private core. Even his wife had to knock before entering. And sometimes wisdom dictated that she just hold her peace and let Tom choose the moment for making revelations. Sooner or later he always did. Nearly always, anyway. Sometimes she'd known him to have a feeling he didn't want to acknowledge because it was so unacceptable to him. Jealousy of Mark probably belonged in that category.

"You won't believe Missy Clarkson tonight," she

said brightly, thinking she was steering the conversation in a safe direction. "She'll never be a fabulous dramatic actress, but when she sings—wow. She was really belting them out today. I think having a real-live professional New York actor on stage with her brought out a talent even she didn't know she had."

Tom set his tea cup down with an alarming clatter. "There's something I wish to hell I didn't have to tell you, but I guess I have to. I suppose Missy didn't know before the rehearsal, but she's sure to know by now."

"What, darling?" Lily asked, all concern. "Is one of the Clarksons ill?"

"In the head, maybe. That damn Jack Clarkson has gone and written a letter to the *Herald* attacking your theater. I walked down to the road because Felipe thought he'd seen a road crew heading this way, and Jimmy Jeffers was just delivering the paper. Told me I ought to look at the editorial page. I did, and stuck the paper away so you wouldn't find it until I got home."

"A road crew," Lily echoed in dismay. The last thing she wanted, with a full house expected that night, was fresh tar on the road and flagmen slowing traffic down to a crawl. For an instant that seemed the bigger news.

"No sign of them," Tom said. "They must have been heading down to Little Springs Road. Believe me, though, you'd be better off with a road crew than with Jack's letter."

"You mean he wrote something against the production?" Lily shook her head incredulously. Father of Missy Clarkson and owner of a large fruit orchard down the road toward Danville, Jack was known for his cantankerousness. It was hard to see how he could object to *Most Happy Fella,* though. True, Rosabella—played by Missy—did get pregnant after a fall from grace with Joe—played by Tibs, but all in the context of a sympathetic story. And the ending certainly made everything right, with a wedding pending between Rosabella and Tony, who said he would love the baby as his own.

Tom was shaking his crop of silver-streaked black curls and saying, "Not against the production, exactly. Worse than that. You'd better read it for yourself." He took the Haiku Valley *Herald,* a thin but locally important two-section weekly, out of the drawer that normally held an assortment of plastic bags and other kitchen wraps. "I thought of hiding it from you," he said, "but then I figured there wasn't any point."

For a wistful split second, Lily wished Tom could have protected her from the letter, at least until after the opening. Even Wonder Woman needed Batman's help now and then. But facts were facts and had to be faced. Anyway, she glowed with pride at Tom's unstated message that she could handle the letter, however unpleasant it might be. She *was* strong, especially here in her temple of serenity, with Tom's face showing love and concern.

Then all her thoughts were focusing on the printed words in front of her.

To the editor:
The time has come for all concerned citizens of

the Haiku Valley to band together to save this place we love. Some of you may remember when our neighbor to the south, Napa Valley, was a beautiful, peaceful region, dedicated to the honest cultivation of the vine. Napa is now the state's second-biggest tourist draw, surpassed only by Disneyland. To a greedy few, it's a gold mine. To most, it's a nightmare. We must not let Haiku Valley go the same route!

Tasting rooms may seem like a reasonable way for winemakers to pull in a needed few extra dollars, but some of our local tasting rooms are turning into three-ring circuses. I don't have to name names. You know who you are, and everyone else does, too. I'm thinking particularly of one vineyard whose so-called new-music concerts attract a crowd of weirdos from San Francisco—the sort who use the rest rooms in our local eating places but don't have the manners or the money to buy a meal. Then there's the tasting room that's turned the area into one big parking lot by inviting "big time" stars to take part in its theater productions. Granted there's a lot of local acting talent that deserves a showcase, but why not leave it at that? Big cities don't offer rural beauty, and country villages don't have to offer "big time" culture. To add insult to injury, this theater is now producing a play about Napa Valley. Get the hint, folks?

Well, some of us don't want to take it. We're forming a group called Against Napa Valley Imitation Locally—ANVIL, for short. Anyone

interested in joining should get in touch with
Buck Olly at Buck's Valley Store or with me
over at the orchard.

Jack Clarkson
Clarkson Orchards, Danville

Making a face, Lily put down the paper. "They
should have picked a more honest acronym—like
Curmudgeons Reacting Against Beauty." She let a
smile flower on her face, though she could see that
Tom wasn't the least bit amused. "Really," she went
on, "that's the silliest letter I've ever read. I can't
believe anyone will pay it a moment's attention. Poor
Missy Clarkson, though," she added more somberly.
"She's so excited about tonight. Her big debut. Do
you suppose this means Jack and Muriel won't be in
the audience? She'll be crushed. More tea, darling?"

Tom merely stared at her. "You're worried about
Missy? What about everything you've worked so hard
for? And what about my business? Do you realize that
sixty percent of our wine sales—and close to eighty
percent of our profit—comes from the tasting room?"

"You don't mean you think this letter could hurt
you! Tom, you're a rock in the Valley. People love
and respect you. You've probably won more medals
for your wine in the past couple of years than anyone
else around. Whose wine is the house wine of most
of the restaurants around here? Yours." Chuckling
softly, she went on, "I can't believe that *I* have to
give *you* a pep talk."

"It's not as if there weren't a grain of truth in what
he wrote," Tom muttered.

Lily felt as though she'd been slapped. "You're

saying you think the theater is somehow going to corrupt the Valley? Or that the Venables' musical nights are going to?" She shook her head in disbelief. The theater had been Tom's idea. He'd always seemed as proud of her best productions as he was of his noblest vintages.

"Not the theater, sweetheart," he said hastily. "Or the Venables' set-up, either. But I do feel a tension growing around here, a conflict of values. Remember when that consortium wanted to buy the Danville Hotel and turn it into a spa?"

"Oh, but that was different," Lily protested. "They were going to have nude bathing in the sulfur springs and quack doctors and a bunch of so-called masseuses whose main qualifications were going to be long blond hair and long tanned legs. All going on in a landmark building that happens to be right across the street from the high school. Nobody minds that the Happy Rest Motel is a hotbed of sin, because it's in a tacky shopping district in Haiku. It's not as if people around here are basically narrow."

"Not narrow, just cautious. And protective of a magnificent strip of glorious land. You're right that the same people who tolerate one standard for Haiku demand a different standard for the Valley. Haiku proper is a city. Not New York, granted; but a city. Safely on the other side of the mountain. The people around here shop in Haiku, but they live in Haiku Valley. Live in it and cultivate it and want to pass it on unspoiled to the next generation."

"And don't I want that?" Lily asked softly.

"Of course you do. You're giving something to the Valley, not taking something away from it. But does

Jack know that? Does everyone in the Valley? I think we ought to have some kind of showdown. We can't just laugh off the letter." Pushing aside his teacup, he reached toward the counter and the telephone.

"No." Lily stayed his hand. "You can't. That letter's about me, not about you, and I have a right to react to it in my own way. I'm Wonder Woman, remember?"

"You don't seem to realize that we're in this together," Tom snapped. "This isn't your world of East Coast sophisticates, where husbands and wives lead parallel lives. What concerns you concerns me."

"I still say you're making too much of it," Lily insisted.

"By New York standards Jack Clarkson may be just a hick farmer, but he happens to carry a lot of weight around here. Don't forget that the governor stumped at Clarkson Orchards when he was running for reelection."

"And the governor lost," Lily pointed out, ignoring a loud voice warning her that the crack would infuriate Tom.

"Great," he said testily. "I'm glad that an hour with Mark was all it took to rev up your old New York style of repartee. Why don't you at least pick up the phone and let a little of your sarcasm loose on Jack Clarkson?"

"Stop it!" Lily clapped her hands over her ears. "From Mark I got 'California, California, California,' as if it were some kind of dirty word. Now you're talking the same way about New York. I'm a person, dammit, not a geographical phenomenon. And I don't want to give Jack the satisfaction of getting angry with him. I want to treat that letter like the eminently forgettable thing it is, and get on with the show."

"You—" Tom began, only to be cut off by the ringing of the telephone. Reaching for the instrument, he said, "Hello? Oh, hi, Missy. Yes, she's right here." He passed the telephone across the table to Lily.

Lily's heart took a dive, but she put on a cheery voice. "How's my Rosabella? All set for tonight?"

Missy's answer was a storm of sobs. "Oh, Lily, I'm so nervous. I'll die in front of all those people."

"Honey, everyone's nervous opening night. I've got butterflies in my own stomach. Mark Davenport thought you were terrific, you know. He said working with you was as easy as working with a pro."

"Really?" Missy asked, her voice brightening through her sniffles. "Did he really?"

"Really," Lily echoed, making a mental note to tell Mark that she'd exaggerated slightly in his name— an act he'd no doubt find justified. "So go throw some cold water on your face and have a light early meal the way I suggested, and everything will be fine."

"I don't know," said Missy's quavering voice.

Lilly looked daggers at Tom, as though somehow Missy's nerves were his fault. "Missy," she hazarded, "does all this anxiety have anything to do with a certain letter in the newspaper today?"

Sobs turned to wails. "Oh, he shouldn't have done it. He's my father and I love him, but to have it in the paper today of all days."

"Now, you listen to me, Missy." Lily's voice was low with urgency. "Your father has a right to his opinions, and you have a right to your moment of glory. You've earned the applause you're going to get tonight. I'm sure your father agrees. Didn't his letter praise our local acting talent? That's you, kiddo. And I want you to know that, as far as I'm concerned, your parents are still welcome at the theater tonight. Are you going to come through like the trouper I know you are?"

"Yes." Missy's voice was quavering, but the tears had stopped. "Yes," she said again, and this time Lily heard granite.

She hung up the phone meditatively. "Jack Clarkson should be spanked," she said, glancing at the clock, a wonderfully corny piece of Americana shaped like a green and white watering can. Five fifty-five. In a little more than two hours the curtain would be rising on a stage set of a San Francisco restaurant. Would Missy Clarkson be waiting in the wings to make her entrance as Rosabella the waitress?

"I think she'll come through," Lily decided aloud.

But Tom's scowling face was signaling that he thought otherwise—about everything. "I think you made a big mistake," he said tersely. "Inviting Jack to the theater tonight is only going to enrage him."

"But he should come! For Missy's sake."

Tom put his hands on her shoulders. "Look, sweetie, I could cheerfully knock his block off at the moment, but I wouldn't laugh in his face. I've respected him as a friend, and at the moment I respect him as an enemy. I suggest you do the same."

"Macho games," Lily scoffed dismissively.

"You know me better than that," Tom said, his voice level, but his eyes sparking.

"I thought I knew you inside out." Lily swallowed hard, trying fruitlessly to dissolve the huge lump in her throat. "Now I'm beginning to wonder. And I thought you knew me too well to treat me like an outsider, someone who doesn't understand the ways of the Valley. I've been here seven years, Tom. I didn't just step off a plane from New York."

"Did I suggest that you had?"

"Of course I did meet someone who'd flown in from New York today." Lily fixed her eyes on Tom's, trying to penetrate their sudden opacity. "That wouldn't have anything to do with the way you're treating me, would it?"

The olive eyes glared now. "I resent that. Why do I get the feeling you want me to be jealous of Mark? I thought your ego was stronger than that."

"Of course I don't want that. I think jealousy is ugly. But if it's there, I'd rather have you admit it than pretend you're above it. At least we'll know where we stand then."

Tom gestured dismissively. "Why don't you just accept the idea that I'm the authority on my own inner workings?"

"Oh, I see. You're allowed to tell me how I'm supposed to feel about Jack Clarkson, but I'm not allowed to comment on your feelings. Seems to me there's a good old-fashioned double standard at work here." Lily took a sip of tea, then disgustedly put down the too-cool cup. "Speaking of work," she added with stiff formality, scraping back her chair, "I want to check on things in the theater kitchen. As you may remember, I'm not only putting on a play tonight, I'm also feeding a hundred people."

She stood up and would have turned away, but Tom got hold of her arms and made a statue of her.

"Talk about a double standard," he said, matching ice with ice. "You're willing to forgive Jack Clarkson for trying to destroy your theater, but you're furious at me for trying to help save it."

"If that's how you see things, it's your privilege." Lily felt as if her eyes were smoking. "I really have to go."

Tom released her without a word. Silence hung heavy in the air as she left the room.

So much, she thought bitterly, for perfect contentment in her kitchen.

6

WALKING DOWN THE STEEP, winding gravel path that
led from the house to the tasting room and theater,
Lily tried to change her mood. As a young actress
she'd learned that it was possible to feign any state
of mind—and, feigning it, to feel it. Love, anger,
lust, depression, giddy good humor, fear, and hope:
All were stored within her, ready to be conjured up
on a moment's notice.

But her anger at Tom had been as strong as it had
been sudden, and it would not yield to her mental
manipulations. Was any anger as deeply felt as the
sort that arises from hurt inflicted by a loved one?
Probably not, she decided. It permeated her every
pore, putting lead into her normally springy step, set-
tling in her stomach like a stone, coating her skin with

an unpleasant clamminess, and imparting a taste of dust to her mouth.

She knew couples who thrived on their fights. Tom's younger sister, Gwen, and her husband, Archie, had broadly hinted that their fights led directly to the bedroom. Lily's sister, Dorrie, had confided that she found arguments with her various beaux "fun" and "growth-enhancing." And Jack and Muriel Clarkson, two people all too much on her mind at the moment, were forever fighting in public—and were clearly one of those couples as strong and eternal as bedrock.

For Lily and Tom, though, fights were as painful as they were rare. Their bouts of anger had the terrible power to turn life upside down in a flash. Love, normally lavished between them, was suddenly withdrawn. No matter how persuasively Lily reassured herself that the love was still there, only its outward manifestation missing, she was in agony. The coldness Tom showed toward her and the coldness she felt in herself seemed the abiding reality. Right now she found it nearly impossible to believe that she and Tom would laugh together again, sling their arms around each other again, be the most stalwart of comrades and the most enamored of lovers.

Her frustration mounting, she kicked at the gravel path, sending a shower of stones and dust into the air. The childish gesture brought little relief from the tormenting questions her mind kept hurling forth. Why did these fights always come at such beastly times —moments when she or Tom or both of them needed an undivided heart and all their internal strength? Why did the fights always start over issues that should have brought them together instead of driving them apart?

The classically thorny issues never bothered them at all. When they'd met for the first time, in New York, it had been apparent to them both that what they felt was really love. Though each of them bore emotional scars, they hadn't had to woo each other or struggle with their own natures before declaring their feelings. And once the words of love had been spoken, they'd both instantly recognized that marriage, and marriage alone, would be the proper framework for their union. Nor had there been any struggle over where to live. Moving to California had seemed a plus, not a minus, to Lily.

The children? Now there was a rocky road in many second marriages, but not in Lily and Tom's. They'd accepted each other's offspring with a genuine fullness of heart. Their attitudes about child rearing had dovetailed from the start, as though the same books had formed both their theories. In fact, both of them eschewed child-rearing books: thus, perhaps, the harmony.

Virtually every fight had been over something or someone external to the marriage—rival candidates for the United States Senate; whether Wagner or Verdi wrote the greater operas; the inherent beauty (or lack of inherent beauty) in football. Through a mysterious process Lily couldn't begin to fathom, the disputes had inexorably turned personal and incredibly hostile. As in today's icy exchange, Lily and Tom had ended up staring at each other over a vast chasm. And, always, Lily had endured an unbearable moment of wondering when and how the two of them would ever come together again.

But she'd never wondered *if* they would come together again, she reminded herself now as she approached the theater entrance. In her deepest heart a core of faith had remained, inviolate under a web of fear and doubts. And this dispute—this *ridiculous* dispute, she lectured herself—would also be dispelled, like morning fog vanishing beneath the California sun.

But when, damn it? Even a minute of this pain was much too long. She thought of a mathematician friend who'd taught her that there wasn't just one infinity; there were greater and lesser infinities. These awful passages never really did last terribly long, yet each one was an infinity.

Thinking she heard a noise behind her, she turned, hoping to see Tom hurrying down the path, a conciliatory smile on his face. But no one was there. She must have heard a car out on the highway. Why should Tom make the first move, anyway? As far as he was concerned, she speculated, he'd only been trying to be supportive—and had received a slap in the face for thanks.

Drawing breath, Lily consciously rearranged her expression. She might not have perfect control over her interior, but she was still actress enough to present exactly the exterior she chose to present.

Entering the theater, she felt an unforced smile warming her face. Really, this was a jewel of a place. Seating just a hundred people in a semicircle, the theater boasted a stage that many a larger, slicker playhouse would have envied. Best of all, sliding doors behind the stage provided unique magic by opening onto a vista of vineyard and hills. Under the illumination of professional floodlights, this glorious specimen of nature's handiwork became a backdrop for the stage. Lily had used her special scenery in such diverse productions as *A Midsummer Night's Dream*, with its forest setting, and *The Chalk Garden*, a drawing room drama in which the windows of the set traditionally hint at greenery beyond.

In *Most Happy Fella*, the vineyard backdrop would be put to its ultimate use. Her production might fall a tad short of Broadway slickness, but no doubt many a New York set designer would envy the breathtaking reality of Gewurztztraminer vines with their bright, beautifully shaped leaves. The Great Designer was even contributing a full moon, which—if the cloud-free sky prevailed—would rise up over the hills and be visible behind the vines during the climactic third act.

Up in the office, the ringing of the phone punctuated her thoughts with a pleasant insistence. Feeling a kind of grim satisfaction, she bet herself that Jack Clarkson's letter in the *Herald* was producing a backlash. Publicity was publicity, and she might very well end up having a full house for every night of the play's run.

Mark Davenport's appearance in Elgin Ives's place would probably have the same effect. Cleo and Tibs were driving all over the valley for her, festooning *Most Happy Fella* posters with banners announcing the change in casting. Lily was virtually certain that no ticket-holders would take her up on her money-back offer. Probably some people who'd been ambivalent about seeing the musical would now feel roused to attend. Something about a change in billing stirred the imagination. After all, theatrical history was filled with tales of understudies who'd shot to stardom when they'd subbed for ailing stars. Mark Davenport wasn't an understudy—and Elgin Ives wasn't quite a star—but they fit into the romantic pattern, anyway.

Lily let her critical glance sweep over the stage. Momentarily satisfied, she decided to check in at the office before visiting the kitchen. She wanted to confirm that she'd been right in her hunch about the nature of the nonstop telephone calls.

As Lily walked into the office, Florence Drew, her box-office manager, tried hastily to conceal something. Lily smiled knowingly.

"The *Herald?*"

Plump, matronly, innocent-looking Florence blushed. "I should have figured you'd have seen it by now. I swear, Lily, I'll never buy another apple or pear from Jack Clarkson as long as I live. But it hasn't hurt us a bit. Aside from a couple of cranks, all the calls have been—" She interrupted herself to answer the phone. "Pennyroyal Theater-in-the-Vineyards. May I help you?" Smiling triumphantly, she went on, "I'm sorry, we're sold out for tonight and tomorrow, and all I can give you for Sunday is three separate singles. No, we're dark on Monday, I'm afraid, but I can give you three very good seats together for Tuesday. Excellent. Curtain at eight o'clock. Our buffet is served from seven to curtain time, with cheese and fruit available during intermission, and dessert and coffee after the show. That's right, it's all included. We'll have the tickets here in your name, Dr. Sanford. Yes, I quite agree. They never should have printed it. Excuse me, Dr. Sanford, my other line is flashing."

The other line went dead as soon as Florence pressed the button. She looked triumphantly at Lily. "That was Dr. Sanford from Little Springs. Isn't he the one who takes care of all those rock stars who have hideaways up there?"

"I think you're right," Lily said. She dropped gracefully down onto Florence's crowded desk. "But Florence?"

"Yes, lovey?"

"I'm not about to tell you what you should or shouldn't say, but I want you to know I'm glad the *Herald* published Jack's letter. Censorship is a far more dangerous business than nasty letters."

Florence waved a bracelet-laden hand dismissively. "I'm not talking about censorship, lovey. But that letter was libel if ever I saw it. I hope you're going to sue the dickens out of Mr. ANVIL Clarkson."

"Sue!" Lily echoed, shocked. "Oh, never, Florence. My father was a civil-liberties lawyer, and he brought me up on Justice Black's belief that there shouldn't be any libel laws at all, much less the loose sort we have today. The First Amendment guarantees about freedom of speech are absolute, and that's all there is to it. If—" She broke off as the phone rang yet again.

"Pennyroyal Theater-in-the-Vineyards," Florence said peppily. "May I help you? I'm sorry, we're sold out for tonight and tomorrow."

Easing off Florence's desk, Lily mouthed, "Kitchen." She cut across the small entrance lobby into a large open space where two young men, Luis

Cayano and Dennis Hoffman, were setting up the long aluminum tables that would soon bear gay grape-pattern cloths and a brilliant array of delicacies.

The room had been built adjoining the tasting room, and the common wall was an accordion affair that would be opened when the crowd arrived that evening. On the far side, Lily could hear the unmistakable resonances of Tom's voice. She tensed. She clenched her fists. Part of her longed to run to him, to dispel the anger between them; part of her went on being affronted.

"Hey, Lily," Dennis called, catching her attention.

Luis nudged him—clearly a signal for him to keep quiet—and Lily instantly knew what was coming.

"That letter from Jack Clarkson was a lulu, wasn't it? I think you should have a sign on the table tonight saying, 'We don't serve any products from Clarkson Orchards.'" Dennis smirked.

"Now, listen," Lily began sternly, "the only thing I intend to do about that letter is ignore it, and I hope you'll do the same. We'll have Clarkson Orchards pear chutney on the table tonight, the way we always do. Jack may not appreciate what I do here, but that isn't going to stop me from appreciating what he does there. And, for heaven's sake, Dennis," she added, "don't say a word to poor Missy tonight."

Dennis and Luis nodded solemnly. Respectively an automobile mechanic and the co-owner of a small but successful pottery shop, both men possessed strong singing voices and were making their stage debuts in *Most Happy Fella* that evening.

"I know you'll be sensational," Lily went on in a warmer voice.

As if on cue, Dennis and Luis belted out the refrain from "Standing on the Corner Watching All the Girls Go By," which they would be singing as part of a quartet of Napa Valley vineyard workers.

Lily felt a grin split her face. Blowing kisses to the two baritones, she pushed open the swinging door to the kitchen.

To her considerable relief, no one in the kitchen had read Jack Clarkson's letter. At least no one chose to mention it. The air was filled with a pleasant frenzy of food talk, matching the medley of deliciously contrasting smells in the air.

"You've outdone yourselves, I can tell just by sniffing," Lily said to her hardworking crew.

Francesca Alexander, the slim red-haired chef, looked up from the dill she was deftly snipping. "I have extra motivation," she said with a merry smile. "Gideon came home yesterday, and he's going to be at the opening tonight. After two years of living in France, he's going to have one demanding palate!"

Lily forgot the swirl in her own mind long enough to absorb Francesca's news. Gideon was Francesca's twin and, along with her, heir to the largest and best-known vineyard in Haiku Valley. Lily, Tom, and a few of their friends on the winemaking circuit had reservations about the Alexander Cellars, but there was no denying they were a force to be reckoned with. The elder Alexanders made clear their own feelings about their status. Their home was a recreation of a famous Loire Valley Château, and its thick stone walls were definitely a signal to keep out. Though they entertained distributors and nationally known wine writers, they had no tasting room open to the public,

nor did they participate in the friendly monthly professional tasting lunches held by the other local winemakers.

Francesca and Gideon had always been different
from their parents, however. Though they could have
coasted through life on their trust funds, both had
instead thrown themselves into their chosen work.
Francesca, who liked to say she'd been born with a
measuring spoon in her mouth, had attended a series
of ethnic cooking schools since her graduation from
college two years earlier. For the past four summers
she'd worked in Lily's theater kitchen, starting as an
apprentice but quickly moving to the head position.
Lily credited Francesca's respect for fresh produce
and her innovative ways with meat and fish for the
success of the pre-theater buffets.

As for Gideon, he'd attended the Davis School of
Viticulture, where Cleo would be a freshman in the
fall. Then he'd gone off to France to work with the
legendary winemakers of Burgundy and Bordeaux.
He hadn't once come back to California to visit in all
that time, though rumors about him had floated across
the sea . . . something about an involvement with the
daughter of one of the French wine barons. Lily was
curious to see what he'd become. Musing on the Alexanders as she stood in the kitchen, she couldn't hold
back an eerie feeling that Gideon was going to play
a role in the life of the Langdon family. Then again,
as she often told Tom, she was blessedly free of any
illusion that she had powers of precognition.

Meanwhile there was the buffet to think about.
Jennifer Berger, one of Francesca's assistants, was

darting from counter to refrigerator and back again to fill a sampler plate for Lily.

"Enough!" Lily begged as Jennifer went back to the refrigerator and added a jellied baby lamb chop to the tempting array.

But as Lily tasted one delight after another, she forgot that she'd just had tea—and that she was in the middle of a stomach-clenching fight with Tom, to boot. The cold salmon had been poached in a stock made of salmon heads, Chardonnay, and a bouquet of herbs from Lily's vegetable garden. The flavor was rich enough to make her swoon, especially when she caught a subtle hint of an anise-flavored herb that conjured up memories of the brief but heavenly romp with Tom in the pennyroyal.

"Fennel?" she guessed brightly, blinking back a sudden irrational impulse to weep.

Francesca nodded. "Not too dominant?" she asked anxiously.

"Perfection," Lily assured her. She heaped similar praise on the bite-size lamb chops, veal and duck pâté with pistachio nuts, and assorted vegetable dishes. Who'd have thought the homely kohlrabi could ascend to stardom in the vegetable kingdom with the addition of a little heavy cream and some snippets of dill? It helped, of course, that the kohlrabi in question had been uprooted only that morning and simmered brief minutes under Francesca's watchful eye.

Kohlrabi was one of Tom's favorite foods, damn him. And one that he hadn't even known about until Lily moved to California and discovered she had a bent for gardening.

They'd learned so much from each other. They had so much yet to learn. If only they didn't have these chilling passages that put thousands of miles between them!

"Is there something wrong with the kohlrabi?" Francesca asked anxiously as Lily paused in mid-bite.

"Oh no, it's heavenly," Lily answered reassuringly. Putting down her plate, she added, "My mind is in a thousand places, that's all. Congratulations, everyone. You've outdone yourselves. I'm sure Gideon will agree you'd get three stars from Michelin if this were Paris."

Protesting that she couldn't possibly taste the desserts and would try them all later, Lily left her devoted kitchen staff. Her heart in chaos, she headed back to the house.

7

AN HOUR LATER, Lily's mirror reflected a woman who considered triumph her due. Everything about her, from her unadorned earlobes to the crisp, classically cut wine-red dress to her red and black Italian kid slingbacks, spoke of purpose and certainty. She worked with her lip brush for a moment, adding glimmering color to her mouth, then gave her sleek dark hair a final brush and toss. The mirror applauded. All that was missing was the laurel crown.

"Liar," she told her reflection.

About her production she had no doubts. She and her cast would earn their laurels. But the theater wasn't the most important element in her life. Her family was. And no one was about to give her any prizes in the domestic-relations department. She'd managed to alienate Tom—and over what? She could scarcely recall the details of their dispute. She only knew that she'd come full circle from anger to guilt. Their fight might not have been entirely her making, but she could have, should have, unmade it. In a flash she remembered a potential fight at breakfast that Tom had lovingly short-circuited by laughing at himself. She owed him one; but instead of setting everything right between them, she'd wasted precious time cherishing her hurt and rage.

She hadn't exactly been the world's greatest mother that day, either. She'd self-indulgently cut off a conversation with Cleo just when the girl was making important revelations, asking big questions.

Lily put down her hairbrush. She looked at her watch. She liked to be at the pre-theater buffet in time to greet the first arrivals, but tonight she had another priority. She was going to find Tom and make peace, by heaven, no matter how late she arrived at the theater. She'd offer Cleo some reassurance, too. With the chameleon Mark in town, Cleo had the right to know that her mother was solidly on her side.

"Now you're in business," she told the Lily in the mirror.

Walking down the hall to Cleo's room, Lily found her daughter sitting in front of her mirror, brushing her lustrous, dark hair. Struck by the echo of her own actions, Lily made herself bite back any comment. Cleo was Cleo, not a replica of Lily, and rightfully resented being reminded at every turn how much she looked like her mother.

"Hi, gorgeous." Lily dropped a kiss in Cleo's hair. "Mmm, something smells terrific. Don't tell me you washed your hair again. You're going to cause a one-woman draught."

Cleo giggled at the familiar tease. "Only twice today. That's not compulsive or anything, is it?"

"Oh, no. Not at all. What are you wearing tonight?" Lily asked.

Cleo stiffened slightly, and Lily prepared herself to hear: "Jeans." Every time Cleo went clothes shopping, she came back with something exotic that just hung in her closet and something denim that became part of her daily wardrobe.

"I think I'll wear that embroidered dress Aunt Dorrie sent from Acapulco," Cleo said. Coloring, she added, "I don't want Daddy to think I look like a hick."

"You could never look like a hick," Lily said indignantly, giving Cleo a fierce hug. "But I'm glad you're wearing that dress. With your red sandals?"

"No," Cleo returned sarcastically, "With my blue running shoes."

Mother and daughter burst out laughing.

"You won't forget we have a date for lunch tomorrow?" Lily said.

Cleo looked up at her. "You really meant it?" Her blue eyes were bright with pleasure.

"Of course I meant it." Lily gazed fondly at her daughter, then let her eyes wander over the inevitable teenage chaos of the room. Someday Cleo would part with her ragged teddy bear and her frayed posters of rock musicians, and someday she would have enough self-confidence to realize how much love she inspired.

Impulsively Lily added, "I have to talk with Tom

before I go to the theater, and I may be a while. You look all but dressed. Do you think you could stand in for me as hostess?"

"Even if I wear my running shoes?"

Cleo's question didn't mask her delight in her mother's invitation, and Lily grinned her own delight. "Even if."

Hurrying down the blue-carpeted hall toward the stairs, Lily crossed her mental fingers. Let peacemaking be as easy with Tom, she prayed. She began rehearsing overtures to him, when the sound of his footfalls on the uncarpeted back stairs drowned out her thoughts with a louder music.

Tom surveyed her coolly as they met on the landing near the top of the stairs.

"Hello," was all he said.

"Hello," Lily said softly, inhaling his essence. He was still in his work clothes and gave off that earthy bouquet she loved—including, she would have sworn, a hint of pennyroyal. "How do I look?"

"You look perfect," Tom returned instantly. "You always look perfect." His lips curled, and he seemed to want to say more, but instead he just repeated his visual survey, letting his eyes linger on Lily's nipped-in waist and well-defined bust before they returned to meet her eyes.

"Tom—" she began.

"I've got to get to the shower," he interrupted. "I don't want to be late for your event. Assuming, of course, that you want me there tonight?" he added gratingly. "Or am I the one person in Haiku Valley who doesn't get the welcome mat?"

Oh Lord, Lily thought, did I hurt him that horribly?

She reached out her hands. "I'll not only put out the welcome mat for you," she said huskily, "I'll also be your doormat if you want."

Tom stared incredulously at her, wiping his dust-streaked brow with the back of his hand. "Did I ever ask you to be my doormat?" he asked softly. "Is that what you think I want from you?"

Mutely Lily shook her head. "Not at all," she finally said. "It was just my way of letting you know that I'd do anything—*anything*—to break this dark spell someone put on us. I want you with me tonight, and I want you with me in spirit. I hate these fights," she went on passionately. "They're like the wars we read about in the papers sometimes—nobody can remember what the original grievances were, or figure out who's right and who's wrong, and the killing goes on and on."

"Such a tender soul," Tom said, a small smile on his face. Gently mocking, he added, "If this is your idea of war, I hope you never have to know what the real thing is about. It would take more than your gorgeous face to win a truce."

"You mean I've won my truce?"

"I don't like fighting any more than you do, Lily," he said. As she let out a sigh of relief, he added, "But let's not have a false peace, either. Nothing's more dangerous. We still disagree about how to handle Jack Clarkson." His voice softening again, he went on, "But ultimately we want the same things, don't we? Your theater to survive, good will to prevail in the valley—and, most of all, having each other."

Lily swallowed hard. "Most of all," she echoed.

"I do love you," Tom said. His face seemed to

lose its angularity as his eyes warmed with unmistakable tenderness. The next minute he was swaggering
again, giving Lily a firm pat on the derriere and saying, "Don't worry, I didn't leave any finger marks.
No one will know that Lady Chatterley stopped by the
gamekeeper's cottage on her way to the theater."
Whistling, he was off to their bedroom and a shower
before Lily could say a word.

Her heart singing, she hurried downstairs and made
her way more cautiously along the gravel driveway.
The slingbacks she was wearing showed off her slender ankles and supple calves but did precious little to
aid her mobility. By now, she supposed, Cleo was
greeting the early arrivals at the buffet. She'd heard
her daughter shut her bedroom door and tiptoe down
the front stairs from the upper hallway, doing her best
to be discreet as Lily and Tom worked out their truce.
Eager to leave Cleo her period to reign, Lily skirted
the main entrance to the theater and went around to
the stage door.

Tibs, who was doubling as stage manager, was
presiding over the green room where the members of
the cast were assembled in various states of readiness.
Inhaling greasepaint, coffee, and an ineffably nos-
talgic aroma of theaters everywhere, Lily hurried over
to her stepson.

"Is Missy here?" she asked anxiously.

Tibs shook his head. "I was just going to call you
up at the house. Everyone else is here. Dennis and
Luis were looking nervous, and Mark got them doing
some breathing exercises. He's okay," he added
grudgingly, as though he hated to concede positive
qualities to his father's predecessor in Lily's life. "Do

you suppose Missy's hung up about that dumb letter Jack wrote? Did you see the silly thing?"

Lily impulsively hugged her lanky stepson. "Thank God someone else sees that letter the way I do. I'm afraid it was a real blow to Missy, though. She called me earlier, and she was crying so hard she could scarcely talk. I thought I got her to put the letter in perspective, but now I'm not so sure. I'd better call her."

Going out to the office, Lily heard the bubbling laughter and raised voices of a happy crowd. Clearly everyone was enjoying Francesca Alexander's delicacies and anticipating an exciting evening of theater. Lily cast up a fervent hope that Missy wouldn't succumb to misery over her father's letter and provide the crowd with more excitement than they expected— a play without a leading lady.

She was so nervous dialing the Clarkson's number that she had to press the disconnect button and start again. Busy. She counted to a hundred and dialed again. Busy. She walked over to the wall and read the rave review one of the San Francisco papers had given to her production of *Fiddler on the Roof*. She dialed. Busy.

She called the operator and asked her to verify the busy signal. The operator reported back the number appeared to be out of order.

Or off the hook, Lily thought grimly. If Jack Clarkson wanted anger from her, he was beginning to get his wish. Not because of what he'd done to her but because of what he apparently was doing to his daughter.

Sticking her head into the crowded room where the

buffet was being held, Lily assured herself that everything was going perfectly in the food department. She
saw Cleo, very much in charge, and very beautiful in
her Mexican dress, pointing out to Jennifer Berger
that a salad bowl needed refilling. Trailing Cleo was
an interesting-looking young man with a decidedly
smitten look on his face—someone from the East
Coast on vacation, judging from his well-cut navy
blazer. Maternal concern suddenly blotting out all other
thoughts, Lily took a step closer to get a better view
of the young man.

Good heavens. It wasn't a stranger at all, it was
Gideon Alexander. Trying to decide whether that
should make her feel more or less concerned, Lily
was interrupted by greetings from a stream of neighbors.

"The lamb chops are fantastic," Florence Drew
gushed. "Is this a crowd, or is it?"

Phil Strauss, the balding retired cantor who'd starred
in *Fiddler on the Roof,* marveled at the Gewurtztraminer Tom and Cleo had selected as the white wine
for the evening. "And don't let that *cockamehmeh*
letter in the *Herald* throw you," he added, his light-
gray eyes dancing. "You do know what *cockamehmeh*
means, don't you?"

"What Cleo would have called 'off the wall' in her
punk phase," Lily answered with a grin. She kissed
Phil's smooth pink pate.

Waving at the crowd, excusing herself to her friends,
she dashed back to the green room. One look at Tibs's
frantic face told her her fears were confirmed: No
Missy.

Impulsively she knocked on the door of the tiny

but well-appointed room with the traditional gold star on the door.

"Come in," Mark called out.

For a moment Lily almost didn't recognize him, so thoroughly had he transformed himself into the unglamorous Tony. In place of the raffish mahogany locks was a head more bereft of hair than Phil Strauss's, and what hair there was had the color and texture of cooked oatmeal. The face beneath the oatmeal fringe had somehow plumped and aged and reddened, suggesting a benign simplicity and an outdoor occupation. The outsize pants Lily had provided were convincingly padded. A short-sleeved white shirt, clean but utterly unstylish, added the final right note.

"You like-a?" Mark asked, putting on a broad Italian accent.

Lily, who hated anything even approaching an ethnic slur, cringed. She had directed her cast to drop any ideas they might have of playing *Most Happy Fella* with the Italian accents of the original production. Fully half the population of Haiku Valley was of Italian ancestry, including her own husband; and she hadn't wanted to risk offending anyone. A fat lot of good her sensitivity had done, she thought bitterly, feeling a wave of genuine resentment toward Jack Clarkson.

But this was hardly the moment to lecture Mark. She knew his public comportment would be impeccable. Anyway, she needed his help.

"I don't think Missy Clarkson's going to show up," she blurted.

Mark's eyes went to the clock on his dressing table. Thirty-four minutes to curtain time. "God save me from amateurs," he said with a groan. "Terminal stage fright? The kid has talent, but she's green, green, green."

Lily wanted to scream, but she held her emotions in check. "Hold off on the lecture," she pleaded. "We've got to figure out what to do."

Mark applied a streak of dark pankcake down the middle of his nose, making it look wider and flatter. "Get the understudy dressed," he said impatiently. "What else do you do?"

"I never have understudies," Lily said, drawing a deep breath. "It's just too unrewarding for someone to learn a big role and then never get to play it."

Turning from his mirror, Mark groaned again. "Lily, Lily, what are you doing in a set-up like this? Doesn't this drive it all home? You belong in the real world. Come back to the New York stage. Act, direct, whatever. A woman with your talent deserves to be surrounded by other pros."

"Mark, stop it! The curtain's going up on a full house in half an hour. This isn't the moment to discuss my life!"

Suddenly his mood turned magnanimous. "I'll tell you what I'm going to do," he said, pushing up imaginary sleeves in the manner of the old Sid Caesar routine. "I'll do my one-man show. The one I've been putting together for Broadway. Frankly, I think your audience will be luckier—"

"Lily?" Tom's strong voice broke into their conversation.

She turned to see him hurrying down the hall from the green room. Even in her anxiety, she noted he'd taken extravagant care with his appearance. Sleekly shaved, his black and silver curls tamed yet still majestically leonine, he was wearing an open-necked green and blue tattersall shirt, a flax-color silk and linen sports coat they'd bought together in Hong Kong, and fine khaki pants that Mrs. White had pressed to a fare-thee-well. He'd taken special trouble to make her feel good, her rapidly beating heart told her. If only she could just link arms with him and set about enjoying a triumphant evening.

Mark was getting to his feet, holding out a hand. "Tom. Good to see you again."

"Happy to make your acquaintance, Tony," Tom returned, pulling out a refrain from *Most Happy Fella*.

Lily's heart swelled. She'd kept a copy of the script by her bedside ever since rehearsals had begun, and Tom apparently had been dipping into it. All tensions between them momentarily swept aside, she thought how like him it was to be interested in her work, quietly interested.

Formalities done with, Tom put an arm around Lily's shoulders. "Missy called up at the house. I think she deliberately wanted to reach me and not you. She's not going to make it. She's just beside herself with anguish, but Jack—"

"The reasons don't really matter, do they?" Mark injected. "I've got to get my act together here. I'm going to do my one-man show," he explained to Tom. "I'll open with a song from *Most Happy Fella*, since I'm already in drag, then I'll do a quick change and come right on with the Hamlet soliloquy. I guess even Haiku Valley has heard of Shakespeare, hmm? Then when I've got them nice and relaxed, I'll jolt them with some Tom Stoppard. Believe me, they'll never be the same again."

Tom turned to Lily in bewilderment. "You're scrapping *Most Happy Fella?*"

"No understudy, old boy," Mark said, shrugging, as if the question had been put to him.

"But you know every line of Rosabella's," Tom said to Lily. "You know every line in the play. That's what you're like when you're directing a play. You could step in for any character in that production—for all of them, if you had to."

"Yes," Lily stammered, "but with Tibs playing Joe? How will I ever keep the audience from giggling during the love scenes? And poor Tibs! He's a terrific actor, but to have to make his debut playing opposite his stepmother—wow! And—" A simple gesture in Mark's direction said all that needed to be said about the awkwardness of singing that final love duet with her ex-husband.

"You can do it," Tom said crisply. "You told me you'd directed the love scenes to hint at what happens between Rosabella and Joe rather than making it graphic. Believe me, two minutes into the production and no one in that audience will remember who's who in real life." Turning to Mark, he added, "I'm sure your one-man show is sensational. But you've got an audience ready for *Most Happy Fella* and a supporting cast who'd feel awfully let down if they didn't get to do their bits."

Mark opened his arms and turned up his palms in the eternal signal that something self-evident had just been said. "No question about it. I was just bawling

Lily out for not doing more with her stupendous talent. There's no one who'd rather see her back up on a stage than I would. Of course if you'd like me to do my one-man show tonight and then you step in as Rosabella tomorrow night, I'd be happy to help you out."

Open-mouthed before Mark's display of naked egoism, Lily was momentarily speechless. Then she quickly said, "Missy Clarkson is going to play Rosabella tomorrow night. No doubt about it." Deliberately addressing her words to Tom, she said, "You really think I can do it?"

"You're Wonder Woman, remember?" he said simply.

Lily felt adrenalin course through her body. "I'll do it," she said. "I'll need fifteen extra minutes to put on my makeup and costume, but I think the audience will understand. I'll have someone make an announcement at the buffet. Tom, do we have enough wine out there? Under the circumstances, the more Gewurztraminer the audience consumes, the happier I'll be."

"You're a natural for Rosabella," Mark insisted. "Isn't that what I said all along?"

He'd said no such thing, but Lily just smiled. The last few minutes had been mercilessly revealing. No need to underscore the point.

"It'll be a great night of theater all around," Tom said diplomatically. "I'll make the announcement about the change in cast. Are Rosabella's costumes here, or is there something you need?"

"Everything's in the women's dressing room," Lily said. Her throat felt dry and tight, but she almost welcomed the symptoms of nervousness. They were part of the ritual. "All I have to do is shed about eighteen years."

"At least you don't have to shed any pounds," Tom said.

In a way, it was the most possessive, husbandly thing he'd said since coming into the theater, and Lily felt an inward jolt of satisfaction. There was something reassuringly *normal* about his need to remind Mark just who enjoyed the delights of her body now.

She would come through for him. She would play her love scenes with Tibs and Mark, but she would play them all *to* Tom. Buoyed by the thought, she ran to dress.

8

APPLAUSE AND SHOUTS filled the theater as Lily and Mark sang the last notes of their duet.

"Brava! Brava!" rang out as an exultant Lily stepped forward for a solo bow.

Exhausted, feverish, giddily triumphant, she ran off stage to be clutched by Tom. His wordless embrace told her everything she needed to know, but she wanted words too.

"I was okay?"

"Extraordinary. Extraordinary," he repeated, looking as dazzled as she felt.

Lord, he must really love her, she thought, to derive so much pleasure from her triumph. He must have understood that every projection of passion and affection came from her feelings for him.

"They're calling for you," he said gently, pushing her back toward the stage.

She bowed alone once more, then with Mark, who gallantly kissed her hand. The whole cast assembled a last time to receive the audience's adulation, then the curtain fell for good.

As she creamed off her makeup in the communal dressing room, the other women in the cast clustered around, offering congratulations. She returned their compliments sincerely. There had been real opening-night magic all around, with everyone down to the chorus members rising to the occasion.

More praise awaited her as, in her normal makeup and shirtwaist dress, she joined her audience in the buffet room. Someone pressed a glass of wine into her hand. Someone else ducked into the kitchen to get her a plateful of cold salmon and salads; the audience was on dessert and coffee, but the cast was expected to do serious eating.

Though most of the comments concerned her performance, she privately felt it was her directing that deserved the greater praise. If it hadn't been for the dramatic circumstances surrounding her last-minute appearance as Rosabella, she doubted she'd be getting quite so many plaudits.

She wasn't too self-absorbed to notice that Cleo and Gideon Alexander seemed oblivious to the rest of the world. Cleo came out of her trance only long enough to introduce her handsome young companion to Tom and Mark, who happened to be standing together.

"Have you met my fathers?" Lily heard her say.

Lily watched proudly as Tom circulated throughout

the crowd, finding something to say to friend and stranger. Now and then she saw him shake his head angrily, and she knew the conversation had turned to Jack Clarkson and his unpleasant letter.

Mark, on the other hand, played the part of the visiting star, waiting for people to approach *him*. When the admirers began to thin out, he tried to monopolize Lily.

"Wasn't she great?" he kept saying to people, a proprietary hand on her elbow. "I had to twist this arm to get her up on that stage, and then she stole the play from me."

Though the line received only polite laughter, he seemed unwilling to retire it. Finally Cleo caught Lily's look of desperation and came to the rescue.

"Dad, as long as you're practically inside the winery, I want to give you the grand tour and show you the cooperage. Gideon knows even more about wine than I do, so if you have any questions, you'll really get answers."

"Now?" Mark protested. Then, "Sure, honey. I've always wanted to watch bottles aging. Take me away."

"We'll give Dad a ride home," Cleo whispered as she linked arms with Mark.

We, Lily thought, mentally raising her eyebrows. But she smiled her gratitude, feeling suddenly wiped out and wanting nothing more than to be at home in bed. Cleo must have seen that.

She managed to wrest Tom away from Deborah Cahn and Ted Bennett, owners of Navarro Vineyards in nearby Anderson Valley, producers of the only vintages Tom seemed to admire consistently as much as his own.

"I hate to be a party poop," she mumbled, "but want to take me home?"

"How could I not want to take the star home?" Tom returned. "Will you invite me up for a nightcap?" A glint in his eyes made it clear that there was real ardor behind the joke.

"Only if you promise not to behave," Lily said. Part of her was totally exhausted, but part of her craved him as though they hadn't made love in eons. It had been feeling for him, after all, that had put the juice in her performance. She had succeeded in exciting herself as well as her audience.

By the time they'd said their good nights and gotten home, though, fatigue had drowned out passion. She wanted Tom, but as a strong, warm body to lie against, a pair of arms to snuggle into as she drifted off into well-earned dreams.

"You luscious thing you," Tom said as she stumbled against him on the stairs to the second floor. His hand made lascivious swirls over her hips as he steadied her.

Even before they got to their bedroom, he was attacking the buttons on her dress, shushing her murmured protests as though they were part of a delightful game.

"We could make love right here in the hallway," he said. "Tibs and Cleo won't be home for hours. Listen."

Lily listened, and heard a crescendo of laughter from the theater. At this point in the evening, Francesca Alexander and her crew would be pushing espresso and sweets to bolster those people who had a thirty- or forty-mile drive ahead of them along dark, winding roads. But even with the wine bottles corked, this was clearly an evening when the party was going to last.

"What do you make of Cleo and Gideon Alexander?" Lily mumbled, kicking off her slingbacks.

Tom shook his head. "Tonight I'm not making anything of anyone but you. Lord, do you know how it turned me on to see you up there on that stage, so beautiful and brilliant, and know that I was going to be sleeping with you tonight?"

Lily's ears perked hopefully at "sleeping," but Tom quickly set her straight.

"Sleeping in the metaphorical sense, of course," he murmured, gently pushing her down on the bed and finishing the work of unbuttoning her dress. "Tell me you want me as much as I want you." His lips fastened passionately on her neck, then blazed a trail down her throat.

"I do," Lily whispered. She was telling the truth; her thighs were parting in anticipation even as her eyelids were threatening to close. She thrust her hands into the thicket of Tom's hair, urging his mouth down into the tender valley between her breasts.

Needing no urging, he stripped Lily's gossamer slip down to her waist, then opened her front-fastening bra, leaving her in the state of partial undress he always found so exciting. He deliberately bunched the lace of her slip and teased her nipples with it; as they stiffened and became more sensitive, he soothed them with his lips and tongue.

Moaning, Lily collapsed backward onto the bed.

"Tell me," Tom said urgently.

"Tell you what, darling? Anything," Lily babbled,

scarcely coherent. "I want you. I love you. Lord, I love you."

Flinging off his pale sports coat, Tom hunkered over her. "Tell me I'm the only one."

Lily's eyes opened wide. "Of course you're the only one." She ran tender fingers over his cheeks. "How can you doubt it?"

"The only one ever." Tom's searching lips bruised hers. "Not in the technical sense," he said roughly. "But in every sense that matters."

Lily's mind reeled. In all their time together, he had never before demanded such reassurance. Her body had always told him what he needed to know; he'd said so a hundred times. Her performance tonight must have affected him more deeply than she'd guessed—perhaps than he'd guessed himself. Though her lips had never touched Mark's on stage, she must have succeeded all too well in conveying depths of emotion.

"If I have to tell you, I can't tell you," she heard herself say huskily. "Let me show you."

She expected Tom's eager compliance; instead, he grabbed hold of her shoulders and shook her. "I want words, dammit. I need words. Tell me."

The imp of perversity produced Lily's next line. "I thought you'd banned such needs from our marriage." Seeking to escape the stormy look in Tom's eyes, she buried her face in the pillow. Oh, heaven, of all nights to run into turbulence. When she just wanted to close her eyes and sleep...

There was a thundering silence from Tom that did more to jar her awake than any noise could have done. Turning to look at him, she found his visage a total mask. She reached up. "This isn't the night for a fight."

"I don't want to fight," Tom exploded.

"No, you just want to browbeat me into telling you that I love you in a way I never loved Mark, that you turn me on in ways he never did." Tears flooding her eyes, she went on, "Do you have any idea how it makes me feel to hear you say you need that kind of reassurance? Hasn't every word, every gesture since the day we met gotten the message across?"

"Mark!" Tom all but spat out the word. "What I'm feeling has nothing to do with Mark. It's you I'm talking about."

"Me?" Lily echoed. Suddenly cold in her half-dressed state, she attempted to pull the bodice of her dress around her. Tom's hands covered hers, impeding the action.

"Do you know how it made me feel tonight to realize I was living with a truly great actress?"

Dizzy, out at sea, Lily said, "You told me it turned you on. I thought that was wonderful. It was as though I'd learned my craft so that one night I could make you wild with desire. But—" She gestured her confusion. "All of a sudden you looked as though you wanted to tear me apart. I never saw that in you." Catching her breath, stifling a sob, she added, "I don't think I ever want to see it again."

Tom's chest heaved as he drew in a great breath. "I didn't mean to frighten you, Lily. It came out all wrong. It's just that after seeing your performance tonight, part of me couldn't help wondering how many other times I'd seen you performing."

His strange logic penetrated Lily's somnolent state.

"You mean you wondered if I'd been faking my feelings for you? In bed?"

"And on the ground," Tom muttered. "Lord knows, I've never been blessed with an abundance of modesty. I think I know what my weaknesses are, but I've never seen my strengths for less than what they are, too. I've always known I had to be good for you sexually because you're so good for me. But have I been as good as you seem to be saying I've been? Tonight in the theater I saw the same look on your face that I saw out in the vineyards this afternoon." His resonant voice shaking, he added, "It threw me. Part of me rejoiced, thinking no one else there really knew what that look meant. But part of me felt betrayed." A sheepish grin crossed his face. "The first part was what made me all but attack you in the hallway. The second part made me drive you crazy with questions."

Lily laughed with relief. But even though the dark spell had passed, and Tom was unbuttoning his shirt like any normal husband getting ready for bed, she saw that he still needed to be stroked.

"Next time," she said with mock severity, "make sure that part one of you controls part two. You know why you recognized that look? Because the only way I could project what I needed to project in that scene with Mark was by calling on what I'd felt this afternoon, lying in your arms, looking up at the sky, seeing the whole universe as rosy and thinking it was all for us. I guess it was a pretty cheap acting trick, drawing on my own emotional life so blatantly, but I didn't exactly have a lot of time to get into my role, did I?"

Tom's face showed his chagrin. "Want me to bend

over so you can kick me where I most deserve it?"

"No," Lily said, "I want you to undress and come to bed, so you can kiss me where I most deserve it."

Tom undid the elaborate silver buckle on his belt. "And where would that be, Mrs. Langdon?"

"Why don't you just start with my mouth and keep going until I tell you to stop?" she said. Her body was sizzling with desire now, all thoughts of sleep pushed away. It was as though Tom's unwonted moment of vulnerability had stirred something in her, pressed some special button. She had to know what kind of lover he would be in this mood. Incredibly tender and eager to please—or, by way of compensation for his tender feelings, aggressive and demanding? She wanted him either way. She wanted him both ways.

Naked, Tom rose from the bed, turned on the electric candle atop his plain pine chest of drawers, and closed the bedroom door. The candle provided a soft glow, backlighting him like a work of art.

"Don't move for a minute," Lily murmured from the bed. She freed herself of her stockings, slip, bra, and dress, leaving only a pale-blue satin scrap of bikini panties and her beloved strand of pearls adorning her body. "Michaelangelo," she said. "Bernini. Some sculptor's idea of the god of the grapes. You're one gorgeous man, Tom Langdon."

"You only love me for my body?"

"Judging from your behavior tonight, you have to admit it's in better shape than your mind."

"Now, listen, lady—" The statue raised a hand in warning. "We gods don't take kindly to being mocked."

"Don't you just? Then forget that god business and

come to bed and be my man. You have an act of contrition to perform, remember?"

As Tom crossed toward her, shadows and moonlight played over his body, accentuating the pared-down waist and muscular thighs, making a tantalizing show of his maleness. Once again, Lily had the delicious, unnerving sensation that he was about to take her for the first time. Don't hurt me, she wanted to cry, as though half her age and very much a virgin. Would he be too much for her? Her thighs trembled in anticipation of being tested. Her center heated to the melting point and turned to molten lava.

Silently Tom spread the pillows out on the bed and arranged her body on them. As she reached for him, he shook his head. "Not yet, my darling. I have to earn my way back into your good graces." He bent over and swooped down on her mouth for a kiss so sudden and fierce that Lily gasped. Instantly his lips became as gentle as butterflies, fluttering over her face, whispering against her lips.

"Who are you?" she cried out softly.

"Your husband. Your lover. A stranger."

The answer excited her, and her hips began gyrating, but Tom stayed her motion with a firm hand. "This is my show, lady. I'm not going to be rushed. I sat unmoving through your performance tonight, and you're going to lie still through mine. Now, let me remember my cue. 'Kiss me where I most deserve—'"

Once again his lips danced over hers, then choreographed a merry jig over her chin and down her throat. "Deserving," Tom murmured, "but not the most deserving. And you, beauteous breasts?" Each in turn, Lily's creamy globes received his attention, his mouth kissing spirals up to her aureoles and nipples. "Are you the most deserving?" he asked her left nipple, then her right, burning the question into the exquisitely receptive flesh with hot flicks of his tongue.

"Very, very deserving, but still not the most deserving," he answered his own question.

As his mouth branded kisses all the way down to her navel and below, Lily thought she would go mad with longing.

"Tom, don't make me wait. I want you inside me. Please, darling. Now." Her thighs moved to capture him. "Now."

Unheeding, Tom bestowed a storm of kisses on her thighs. As her moans filled the air, his mouth sought the sweet, secret, innermost flesh of her thighs. "I do believe I've found the most deserving place," he murmured. "And I will give it all that it deserves."

The sudden arching of Lily's back told him he had kept his promise.

"Darling, darling, darling," she cried brokenly from another planet. Swirling lights and velvet blackness owned her mind. The most gorgeous Eden in all the universe, but lonely. "I want you out here with me," she called. Her hands groped blindly. "No place to be alone..."

"Come and get me," said her husband, her lover, the stranger.

Wild energy coursing through her veins, she propelled herself back to earth. With a starved eagerness, she feasted on Tom's mouth. His full lips were like ripe jungle fruit, hot and winey, all but bursting. Her voracious mouth traveled on to other exotic treats: his earlobes, his collarbone, the mysterious pool of his navel. All beckoned to her, but none sated her.

"Yes, yes," Tom moaned, as her banquet continued. "Oh Lord, yes, my Lily."

Triumphant laughter welling deep inside her, she gave her lips and tongue license to bring Tom the ultimate pleasure. But then he turned the tables on her, pulling her gently up until her mouth was on his mouth, her knees on either side of his hips.

"Together this time," he commanded, in a voice that brooked no refusal. But why decline such a gorgeous order? Ecstatic, Lily allowed him to maneuver her rhythmically up and down, fusing them.

Once again she rocketed off into the far reaches of the sky. But this time there was no loneliness, for Tom was right there with her, so absolutely and profoundly linked to her that she hadn't the dimmest notion where she ended and he began. But maybe in the place where they were, endings and beginnings were one. Everything was one. Oh, heaven, what a wondrous business that mere mortal flesh could carry the spirit into rare and mystical spaces. Because in the place where oneness *was,* the body was the spirit. And the name of the place was marriage.

Coming back to something approaching normal a small eternity later, Lily opened her eyes. Tom was awake and looking at her—Tom, her husband and lover, with the stranger nowhere in sight. Not sure whether she was relieved or sad that the stranger was gone, she snuggled into Tom's warmth.

"Feel good, sweetheart?" he asked.

"That might just be the understatement of the year. How about you?"

"Yup," he said, unabashedly smug.

Lily kissed him lightly. Then, unable to resist, she said, "You weren't acting, were you?"

"You—" he began, raising his hand in a mock threat. Then laughter shook his frame. "If I did everything again exactly the same way, would that prove I was for real or a fake?"

"I'll take it under advisement," Lily said, "and deliver my answer tomorrow. By registered mail. I love you, by the way."

"I wish you'd stop beating me to all the good lines," Tom grumbled. He scattered kisses through her dark hair. "Since it can't be improved on, I'll just have to echo it. I love you. By the way." Cocooning her in his arms, he said, "Could I sell you on a little shut-eye?"

Lily, asleep, didn't answer.

9

BREAKFAST THE NEXT morning struck Lily as a triumph of normalcy. It was as though her family of four had always been gathered around that table drinking orange juice and eating scrambled eggs and toast— as though they would always be there. True, Cleo had new stars in her eyes. They were shining for Gideon Alexander, Lily guessed, and she crossed her mental fingers. Cleo had a very innocent side, all too apt to be bruised by the worldly likes of Gideon. But, then, teenage infatuation was part of normalcy, too. Tibs— and the rest of the family—had managed to survive his on-and-off cycles with a series of girl friends. They would survive Cleo's. Romance, with all its complexities, was a glorious fact of life.

A gentle nudging under the table reminded Lily of

the twist her own romance had taken the night before. Returning Tom's pressure with her moccasin-clad foot, she felt a ripple of pleasure in her belly that had nothing to do with orange juice. If only life could always be like this—resonant, reaffirming, challenging, detailed but not boggling.

"Was that someone at the front door?" Tibs asked. "I'll get it."

He returned in a moment, carrying a gift-wrapped box that he handed to Lily. She looked inquiringly at Tom, but he shook his head.

"I wish I could sit here looking guiltily expectant," he said ruefully as Lily undid the blue satin bow, "but someone else beat me to it."

"Who brought it?" she asked Tibs.

"Some guy in a Jeep. Uh—the perpetrator was a Caucasian in his mid to late twenties, with brown hair and two eyes, wearing a denim shirt and jeans." He spread his hands. "Want me to alert the highway patrol?"

Lily laughed. "Maybe I'll just read the card." Taking the rectangular pasteboard out of its envelope, she read aloud: "'A star is reborn.' No signature." But as she undid the silvery paper and saw the familiar box, she had to concede that she needed no signature. The intricate design of lilies of the valley was the trademark packaging of Night Blooming Lilies, the rich, sophisticated scent she'd worn for years—until she'd met Tom. One night when he'd come to her apartment to pick her up for dinner, he'd gently explained to her that winemakers were cranky about perfume, especially when they were eating and drinking. Half of the pleasure of wine was its "nose"—and how could you appreciate it if your own nose was suffused with competing scents?

Lily had poured Tom a glass of Chardonnay from a bottle he'd given her; she'd explained to Cleo and the babysitter that she wasn't going out just yet; and she'd jumped into the shower. Half an hour later, as they embraced in a taxi on their way up to the Italian Pavillion, she'd known that she and Tom would become lovers that night. Before the night had ended, she'd known she was going to marry him. The next day she'd given away a nearly full atomizer of Night Blooming Lilies and hadn't thought about it since.

Clearly Mark had thought about it, though. As far as he'd been concerned during their marriage, she couldn't wear too much of the heady stuff. He used to say that when he was as rich and famous as Richard Burton, he would buy the rights to Night Blooming Lilies so no other woman in the world could ever wear it.

"I guess it's from my co-star," she said brightly to her family.

"Remember he said he brought us 'trinkets from civilization'?" Cleo reminded her. "I bet that was one of them. But you don't wear perfume, do you, Mom? Just that vanilla dusting powder sometimes."

"I used to wear perfume, honey." Lily reached out a hand to Tom, giving him a soft look. "Then I realized it was more fun and more important to be able to smell wine—and for everyone around me to be able to. I guess I can't pass the present on to you, my young winemaker."

"Oh, I wouldn't wear it anyway," Cleo said, wrinkling her nose in best adolescent style. "It's like wearing makeup. Gideon—" The name came out chokily, on the crest of a giggle.

"Ahah!" Tibs pounced. He waved a piece of toast meaningfully. "What have we here?" Then, seeing Cleo's discomfort, he put a brotherly arm around her. "Gideon likes wearing makeup?" he asked blandly, evoking laughter from everyone present and clearing the air.

Tom picked up the perfume box and hefted it. "I thought they only made cologne in this kind of volume. That's some trinket." His eyes dull, he added, "Enough to make up for a lot of lost time. Have you missed it, Lily?"

"Not for a minute," she said honestly. "I'd probably hate the smell now." Reaching for the perfume and putting it on the counter behind her, she said, "It's going to make a wonderful present for someone. Or I'll donate it to the next high school fund-raising raffle. More toast, darling?" she asked Tom.

"I'm fine, thanks. If—"

The telephone cut him off. Lily answered, to be greeted by Mark's famous raspy voice.

"I hope you're going to reconsider about tonight," he said without preamble. "Missy Clarkson has a great voice, but you're a great actress. Give the locals a break, why don't you? You know, I was thinking it's about time for *Most Happy Fella* to be revived on Broadway. If you did the run of the production with me here, we might be able to get some press. Then Chris McWhorter would have some ammunition for facing the big-time money. Hell, we might even import Tibs as Joe. He's got talent, and the publicity angle would be sensational."

Lily glared at the telephone, conscious that her family's eyes were fixed on her. "I'm a director," she told Mark. "And a Californian. Will you please drop this nonsense about the New York stage?"

"You can fool yourself, but you can't fool me," Mark persisted. "You're still a night-blooming Lily."

"Oh, thank you for the perfume," she said woodenly. Something in Tom's face was making her uncomfortable, and she wanted to get off the phone. "Can we talk later, please? I'm being rude to my family, breaking my own rule against talking on the telephone during meals."

Ringing off, she smiled apologetically at Tom and the children. "Everyone always thinks big after a good opening night," she explained. She didn't want to be critical of Mark in front of Cleo. "My co-star apparently woke up thinking about playing Tony on Broadway."

"With you as Rosabella," Tom said tightly.

Lily waved away the thought. "He was just being polite," she said, knowing full well that the words rang hollow. "He also talked about Tibs as Joe," she made a point of saying.

"Cover-up," Tom said brusquely. Then, chagrined, he turned to Tibs and said, "Not to slight your talent, son. I happen to think you were *the* male star last night."

"Indeed you were," Lily said warmly. "I looked good because you made me look good. And you will be on Broadway someday, if that's what you want," she added.

Tibs flushed. "I've been thinking more along the lines of doing rep in San Francisco. Much as I love playing Joe, I'd rather do straight plays than musicals. Maybe some experimental stuff. When I'm ready. I'm not about to drop out of Berkeley. I'm still not sure I wouldn't be as happy as a psychologist. Anyway, it's nice to have options."

"All that talent and practical, too," Tom said. But his look of pride gave way to a more ominous expression as his eyes moved from Tibs's face to Lily's. "Have you been missing New York? Not just the theater but the whole bundle?" More apologetic than angry, he added, "We don't even go to San Francisco as much as we used to. Maybe we should subscribe to the symphony again and give ourselves the motivation."

"That would be lovely," Lily said eagerly.

The telephone rang again. This time Lily was greeted by a long-distance hollowness. The caller identified himself as Richard Pearson, drama critic for one of the San Francisco dailies. A vacationing reporter had seen Lily the previous night and had just called Pearson to rave about her performance. Would she be subbing as Rosabella tonight? If so, said Richard Pearson, he would like to be in the audience.

Lily sighed deeply. "Come review my directing instead," she suggested lightly. "And discover my stepson, Tibs, who's a terrific Joe, and Missy Clarkson. Believe me, she's the one around here who has the voice for Rosabella. I'll be happy to arrange seats for you, even though the house is sold out. No, that has nothing to do with it," she replied in answer to a question from the other end. "Honestly, we don't have a 'divided valley' here, Mr. Pearson."

Hanging up, she explained the call to her family.

Again Tom's face tightened. "Want to bet Mark was the 'vacationing reporter' who tipped him off?" Not waiting for an answer, he said, "I'll be working with the Cabernet grapes. Don't forget about the tasting lunch, Cleo." He strode out of the room.

A loud silence prevailed. Tibs, whistling, stood up and started to clear away the breakfast dishes. Cleo stared wide-eyed at her mother, as if trying to sort out the flying words of the past hour.

"If Dad did call that reporter, it wasn't the worst thing in the world, was it?" she asked uncertainly, clearly caught between two loyalties. "I mean, I can understand why Tom was upset, but I guess no one can blame Dad for thinking you're a great actress."

Lily put a protective arm around her daughter. This was just the sort of tug-of-war she'd hoped Cleo wouldn't be subjected to.

"I do wish Tom and Dad could be friends," she went on.

"Well, they're not enemies," Lily said. "Lots of times when one or both halves of a divorced couple remarries, people actively dislike each other or don't talk to each other or some other really sticky situation develops. Mark and Tom have very different values. It would be nice if they were friends, I agree, but it may be an unrealistic expectation. At least you have the comfort of knowing they both love you, and that's what counts."

"They both love you, too," Cleo said, tossing back her long blue-black hair.

Lily thought for a moment. "It's more that Mark remembers loving me. There's a difference."

"Do you remember loving him?"

"I know that you were born of love," Lily said, her throat catching. "And yet . . ." She shook her head. "I know I must have loved him, yet I can't remember the feeling. Does that make any sense?"

"I think so," Cleo said doubtfully.

"Maybe you don't want to remember," said Tibs the psychology major, turning from the sink. "Maybe you think it would be disloyal to Dad. Really, it wouldn't be, you know."

Lily felt tears prickling her eyelids. How lucky she was to have these two wonderful young people in her life. Probably everything they were saying was true. She just wasn't ready to identify or deal with her feelings for Mark. Eventually she would have to, but when the time was right. Sometimes the mind could be pushed; sometimes it had to be allowed to sift and sort at an unforced pace. Truth was better served that way.

She praised Tibs and Cleo for their wisdom, then said to her daughter, "Did you double-book lunch today?"

Cleo clapped her hand over her mouth. "Oh, Mother, how could I have? When you and I talked yesterday, I forgot that the second Saturday in the month was coming up."

"Never mind, honey. You and I can have lunch almost any old time. I should have remembered myself. You go to Haiku with Tom."

"Why don't you go in my place, Mom?"

"Me?" Lily eyed Cleo, wondering what was going through the girl's mind. There was a faint blush on her cheeks—or was it a reflection of the red plaid shirt she was wearing with her jeans? "Because what Tom said about your father upset you?" Lily guessed.

"Oh, no, not at all. I mean, you're right that it could be a lot worse between the two of them. But until I got interested in wine you always used to go to the wine-tasting with Tom."

"So I did. But mostly just to keep him company." Lily looked over her shoulder. "Tibs, how about putting a flame under the coffee?"

"It's already on."

"Oh, you clever fellow," Lily said with a smile. "Anyway, honey," she went on to Cleo, "you know much more about wine than I do now. You belong there. Unless you have some other reason for not wanting to go?" She eyed her daughter speculatively.

"Here you go, Step-Ma," Tibs said lightly, putting a fresh mug of coffee in front of Lily.

"As in wicked?" Lily returned in the same spirit. But her eyes were still on Cleo.

"Actually," Cleo mumbled, "I was thinking—" She swallowed hard. "Thinking that Gideon might think—" Unable to complete the sentence, she looked at her mother with large, beseeching eyes.

Suddenly Lily felt as though she'd left her own teenage days only moments ago. "You're afraid that if Gideon is at the lunch he'll think you're there because you're interested in him?"

Her face suffused now, Cleo nodded. Tibs quietly began loading dishes in the dishwasher.

"But surely you told Gideon that you're going to Davis in the fall?" Lily probed gently. "So a tasting lunch is a perfectly natural place for you to be."

"Just feels funny," Cleo mumbled.

"He certainly looked plenty interested in you last night. And didn't care who saw it," Lily said.

Cleo lit up like a theater marquee. But she didn't say anything, and Lily gave a resigned sigh. She'd always believed that you had to honor other people's instincts, even if their reasoning seemed strange. And, really, Cleo's thinking wasn't all that foreign to her— or all that off-base, either. Lily felt a lot more comfortable with her daughter's sweet reticence than she would have with wily aggressiveness.

"All right, I'll go to the tasting with Tom, and you and I will have lunch on Monday," she told Cleo. She amused herself by wondering for a moment if Tom would think she'd contrived an excuse to be with him. Well, she hadn't contrived it, but she had to admit she welcomed it. His mood at breakfast had been maddening, moving as it had between sunshine and storm. If only he would come out and admit his jealousy of Mark! But apparently he was no more willing to accept it than she was willing to acknowledge how deep her feelings for Mark had once been. Nothing human was ever simple, least of all where love was concerned.

Somehow they had to get back on the track again. She just hoped Tom was as eager as she to restore their life to what it had been, to bring romance home again. If they stayed at odds with each other, nothing would be right. But if they collaborated, they could have whatever they wanted, no matter how many Mark Davenports and Jack Clarksons put wedges between them.

Tibs sat down next to her, cradling his mug of

coffee in his hands. "I'm Tibs Langdon from *The Los Angeles Lampoon*," he began cheerily, "and we've heard a rumor that you're going to get Missy Clarkson onto a stage tonight. Want to tell us how you're going to pull that off?"

"I'm going to go to her house and talk to her," Lily said, though until that moment she hadn't known what her plan was.

"Want me to ride shotgun?" Tibs offered.

Lily felt her face grow warm as she remembered using the same phrase with Tom after their ardent tryst in the vineyards. "Oh, I'll be fine, Tibs," she said. "You are a love, though."

She didn't tell him the truth, which was that she would have welcomed his company, not out of any fear of Jack Clarkson but just for general moral support. She wasn't about to involve him in an undertaking that Tom would so clearly disapprove of, however. In their years together they'd been very scrupulous about never using their children in their private wars, never asking the kids to take sides.

We fight, but we fight clean, Lily thought to herself.

Cleo sat silent, and Lily wondered what she made of the whole Clarkson mess. Unlike Tibs and Tom, she'd offered neither support nor criticism of Lily. Probably her main worry at the moment was how Gideon Alexander would perceive the contretemps. Cleo did seem to be on the verge of a major obsession with the young man. Lily wasn't sure whether she hoped Gideon was equally full of Cleo at the moment or whether she hoped the relationship went no further. Anything involving the Alexanders was bound to be plenty complicated. Then again, anything involving the human heart was bound to be complicated. And Cleo, for all her innocence and love of the land, wasn't about to attach herself to some Haiku Valley youth who thought that San Francisco was the farthest known point of civilization.

Well, if Lily were going to drive over to the Clarksons' and work some magic on Missy, the time to go was now, before she lost her nerve. Having arrived upstairs to get her purse, she heard the telephone ring and grabbed the bedroom extension.

"Hello, Cleo?" she heard. "It's Gideon. Gideon Alexander."

Realizing Cleo had answered downstairs, Lily gently replaced the receiver. She smiled. There had been an endearing uncertainty in the way Gideon had given his last name, as if Haiku Valley were filled with young men named Gideon.

She distinctly remembered the first time Tom had telephoned her. They'd met briefly at an advertising agency where Lily was auditioning for a part in a California wine consortium TV commercial. Thomas Langdon had been but one of half a dozen winemakers present, Lily but one of a dozen actresses eager to work. Yet something had happened between them: one of those moments of recognition that makes everyone else in the world recede into a foggy distance.

That night Lily had answered her phone and heard: "Lily? It's Tom." No last name had been uttered; none had been needed.

Lily had loved his brashness. Now she liked Gideon's absence of brashness. She supposed she was guilty of having a double standard, of wanting a level of danger for herself and a level of safety for her daughter. But maybe that was the way the species was programmed. She reminded herself to bring up the topic with Tom during one of their halcyon moments.

Bag slung over her shoulder, she made her way downstairs and into the kitchen. Tibs, the soul of courtesy, had vanished, leaving Cleo alone with her telephone caller. At the sight of her daughter, Lily bit back a grin. If ever there were a classic example of teenage body language, here it was. Legs twisted around each other, Cleo had her left elbow propped against the kitchen counter and her right hand alternately caressing the receiver and waving wildly in the air. Desperately curious but not wanting to be intrusive, Lily quickly tiptoed to the door.

"Mom!" she heard as she was about to get into the Datsun. Cleo was sprinting down the driveway, her sun-dappled dark hair flying behind her. "That was Gideon. Guess what?"

Lily smiled indulgently. "I give up."

"He wondered if I would go to the tasting lunch with him!"

"And you said—"

"Yes, of course," Cleo answered.

"Terrific," Lily said. "A double date. Or are Tom and I supposed to keep our distance? Goodness," she added, "I hope Tom isn't too crushed that you're throwing him over for a younger man."

Cleo was too excited to find anything hurtful in the gentle tease. "He'll understand," she said confidently. "He's my father. My step-father," she amended. "You know."

"I do know." Lily kissed Cleo on the forehead.

"You're a wonderful young woman, and Tom and I—and Mark, too—only want you to be happy. I better get going, honey. I'll be back within the hour. If you need to borrow anything from me for the lunch—"

"Gideon says he loves my naturalness. Not that your things aren't, you know—"

"I repeat, I do know. Do you want a lift with Tom and me? Or is Gideon picking you up?"

"I don't need a ride, thanks. Gideon says he'd like the extra half hour with me." Cleo's eyes had the fire of someone who has suddenly been made privy to the secrets of the universe.

Wondering how many sentences she would hear in the next few days beginning, "Gideon says," Lily got into the Datsun, gave Cleo a wave, and set off for the Clarksons'.

10

JACK, MURIEL, AND Missy Clarkson lived in a big stone house atop a gentle hill. At the foot of the hill, where their driveway began, a redwood roadside stand offered the pears, apples, berries, and other seasonal fruit for which Jack's orchards were justifiably famous. Homemade goods were also available, including Muriel's fruit pies and the pear chutney that always adorned Lily's pre-theater buffet tables.

Skirting the public parking lot and heading up toward the house, Lily leaned out the Datsun window to wave at Red D'Addario, who ran the stand for the Clarksons. Looking startled at first, then favoring her with a grin that spread across his big, freckled face, Red enthusiastically returned the wave. Lily felt undeniably satisfied. Despite her avowed and private resolve not to take Jack Clarkson's letter seriously, she hadn't helped but notice at the theater the previous evening who was being extra friendly and who was being somewhat aloof. Even though one voice in her head was calling her petty, she was glad to see that Jack had a dissident on his own turf.

Truly, she dreaded the idea of a divided community. She'd known for some time that there were some Valley folk who weren't thrilled about the theater, but one always had some dissatisfied neighbors. She'd tried to placate hers by expanding the parking lot in front of the tasting room so no theatergoers trespassed on nearby property. She refrained from using resonant instruments or overamplifying the stage, so that even when the back wall of the theater was open to reveal the glorious vineyards, the noise stayed within Langdon property lines.

But admittedly she didn't have a great deal of sympathy for those people who simply didn't want anything going on in the Haiku Valley that hadn't been going on fifty years before. To pretend that the area could prosper independent of tourist business was simply a delusion. Surely Jack Clarkson himself knew that more of Muriel's strawberry-rhubarb pies were consumed by people passing through than by locals. Locals made their own pies.

Most of all, she didn't want a divided household. Blast Jack Clarkson for coming between her and Tom.

Chuckling as she parked the car in front of the Clarkson homestead, she realized how ironic her anger at Jack was. If she'd been angry at him in the first place, she and Tom wouldn't have fought over the letter. She had to admit she no longer saw the letter as simply silly, though she still felt Tom's reaction to it had been exaggerated.

She closed her eyes and tried to project her thoughts into a wonderful near future. The letter business would be resolved, Mark would be back on the other side of the country, and she and Tom would have a world-class marriage again. If only she didn't take the lumps and bumps of married life so seriously! Give Tom another seven years and maybe she wouldn't...

Then again, she'd married him in the expectation of emotional grandeur, an ambition she knew he shared, and she wasn't about to tolerate a lesser life. Give her another seven years, and maybe Tom would see that no rent in the fabric of their intimacy, however slight, could be ignored. She knew all too well from her first marriage that small tears became gaping holes in the blink of an eye.

Well, this was hardly the time and place for meditation. Resolutely she got out of the car, giving the door a good, solid thwack behind her, and marched up to the Clarksons' front door. In country style, it was open, with an unlocked screen door as the only barrier. On other days, she'd just opened the screen door and hollered, "Anyone home?" But a shade more formality seemed in order this morning. She rapped on the blue wooden frame.

Muriel came down the hallway, looking the picture of the pie maker. Mildly plump, she wore her gray hair on top of her head in a knot that was never quite orderly. Her very pale skin was marked with many laugh lines and few worry lines—the sort of skin you saw on the face of someone who was always thinking about other people rather than herself. She was dressed in a shirt and skirt so unremarkable that you could forget them even while you were looking at them.

Because of the tricks the sunlight and screen played with her vision, Muriel didn't realize who was standing outside her door until she and Lily were almost nose to nose.

"Oh, my goodness," she said with a gasp, clapping her hand to her mouth when Lily's face came clear. She put her hand on the knob, then froze, obviously caught between her innate hospitality and the possible unpleasant implications of Lily's presence.

"Don't worry, Muriel," Lily said, smiling. "I won't bite. I just wondered if I could have a word with Missy."

"Come in, come in," the flustered Muriel said. "We can't have you standing out there like a salesman."

Lily doubted that Muriel had ever let a salesman stand on her steps; one local story held that a network of door-to-door vendors had passed the word as far as Washington State and Baja, California, that Mrs. Clarkson served the best pie and coffee on the West Coast.

"Oh, Lily," Muriel said, ushering the younger woman into her fragrant kitchen, "I just don't know what to say."

"You don't have to say anything," Lily answered kindly. "I didn't come to put you—or anyone—on the spot. I just want to talk with a certain very good young actress. Is she around?"

"Yes, but—" Muriel opened one of her professional cast-iron ovens, making the air yet more fragrant, and pulled out a steaming pie with a lattice crust. "Won't you have a cup of coffee and a piece of pie? It's mixed wild berries—raspberries, blackberries, and loganberries. Jack's favorite," she said, and then bit her lip.

"One of my favorites, too," Lily said. "But if I could talk to Missy first, I'd enjoy it a lot more. I'll have some of your wonderful coffee, though," she added, not wanting to offend Muriel.

As Muriel took down a willow-pattern cup and saucer from a cupboard, she shook her head, and Lily could almost see it buzzing with angry thoughts about her husband. Muriel and Jack were famous for their arguments, which were often waged with complete disregard for inadvertent eavesdroppers. But Muriel wasn't about to say a word against her husband behind his back, Lily noted with admiration.

Muriel disappeared upstairs while Lily sipped a rich blend of Colombian and mocha java coffees. From above her, she heard the unmistakable cadences of two females disagreeing with each other, and she guessed unhappily that Missy was balking at facing her. For a moment she considered retreating. She liked Missy, and she truly didn't want to increase her evident discomfort. Then again, Missy wasn't going to show up at the theater without some coaxing. If she missed the run of the play on which she'd worked so hard, she might carry the regret with her for years.

"Muriel?" A loud male voice interrupted Lily's thoughts. "You in the kitchen?"

A moment later Lily was face to face with Jack Clarkson, his face red from sun and hard work, or perhaps from embarrassment. In fact, Lily would have been hard pressed to know whether he or she was the more discomfited.

"Hello, Jack," she said evenly.

"Morning, Lily." He took a bandanna from around his neck and wiped sweat from his brow. "Muriel know you're here?"

"Yes, she does," Lily said. "I'm not in the habit of walking into your kitchen, pouring myself coffee, and sitting down at the table." Her sharp words seemed to tumble out of their own accord, but she had to admit she felt better for having uttered them.

Jack poured coffee but didn't sit down with her, choosing instead to lean against the double stainless-steel sink. "I suppose you're mad about the letter," he said.

"Well, how would you feel, Jack? I thought we were friends, at least good neighbors. If you wanted to complain about my theater, I think you might have done me the courtesy of telling me to my face." Jack looked so uncomfortable, his big, squarish body propped at an awkward angle, that she felt sorry for him. But something made her press on. "Or, if you had to write the letter, you might have held off for a week to give Missy her unspoiled moment of glory. She's a very fine singer and a promising actress, and she should have been on the stage last night."

"I didn't forbid her to go." Jack's facial muscles worked. "I told her to do whatever she saw fit."

"Come on," Lily scoffed. "You know perfectly well that if you didn't forbid her to show up last night, you might as well have. You were obviously the reason she stayed home."

Jack looked downright miserable now, and Lily knew he hadn't foreseen the consequences to his daughter when he'd written his letter.

"I thought they'd run the letter next week," he mumbled. "They're not always so all-fired quick at the *Herald*." Straightening, he added in a defiant voice, "I'm not taking back a word I wrote, mind you. The next thing you know, we'll have billboards on the roads, and the gas stations'll be selling T-shirts and buttons with obscenities on them."

"Oh, Jack." The rattle of Lily's cup against her saucer revealed her impatience. "You know me and Tom. Do you think we want those things any more than you do? But I'll be damned if I can see any connection between a theater featuring local talent and serving local food, and obscene T-shirts. And you can't pretend the Valley doesn't need some economic booster shots, just the sort we're providing. You're the one who brought up gas stations. Well, Randy over at the Cut-Rate told me he might have had to sell his franchise if it hadn't been for the extra business from the Venables' vineyards and ours."

Jack licked his lips. "I've known Randy since he was a baby, and he never could manage anything. You can't convince me we've got a depression here just because Randy can't balance his books. We've got other gas stations doing okay."

"I wasn't talking about a depression," Lily said patiently. "Just about tough times. Maybe the other gas stations are doing better, but I bet none of their owners have rushed to join ANVIL."

"Sometimes people don't know what's in their own best interests," Jack insisted. He gave his dusty jeans a hitch and went to refill his coffee cup. "You'll see," he added obscurely, setting the percolator back on the range with an emphatic thud.

Footsteps sounded on the stairs, and Muriel appeared with Missy in tow, a pale, red-eyed, hollow-cheeked Missy. Lily's heart went out to the girl, whose gaze shifted uneasily from her father to Lily and then away altogether, as though she didn't know which of them made her more miserable. Muriel, on the other hand, frankly glared at her husband.

"You've left Lily with an empty coffee cup," she accused him, as if this were the heinous act that had brought them all together in the kitchen.

"It's all right, Muriel," Lily said. "I've about reached my caffeine limit." She gestured at the chair opposite her. "Come sit down, Missy. As I told your mother, I didn't come to bite anyone. I'd just like to find a way of persuading you to play Rosabella for the rest of the run."

"How can you even talk to me?" Missy whispered, clinging to the door frame. "I let you down so horribly."

Jack shifted uncomfortably. "I'll be getting back to the orchard now. I don't suppose the pie is cool enough for eating?" he added, casting a wistful look toward Muriel's fragrant mixed-berry masterpiece.

"You're not going anywhere, Jack Clarkson." Muriel folded her arms across her chest. Her voice softened. "I think the pie will be ready about the time we have a happy girl again."

Missy looked as though she planned never to be happy again, even though Lily gave her a reassuring smile. "We survived," Lily said crisply. "No one is indispensable to a production, not even a star. We managed without Elgin Ives last night, and we managed without you. But we'd manage better with you," she went on, grinning. "And I think you'd manage better, too. Skipping last night's performance doesn't seem to have done you much good."

"I didn't sleep," Missy said, confessing the obvious.

Jack stared out the window, looking as though he wished a giant bird would swoop down and carry him off. "I didn't tell you not to go," he said defensively.

"Oh, Dad. I would have died of embarrassment. And, I don't know, I really don't agree with anything you wrote in the letter, but I still didn't want to be disloyal to you."

Swallowing hard, Jack crossed the room and patted Missy's straw-blond head. "I really didn't mean for you to be caught in the middle of all this," he said awkwardly. "Especially after all that rehearsing and everything."

"Well, maybe I gave the audience a break," Missy mumbled. "I heard you were a great Rosabella, Lily."

Lily shrugged. "I did a pretty good job under the circumstances. But people wouldn't have thought so much of my performance if it hadn't been for the drama of a last-minute takeover. Anyway, I never could sing, Missy. You have a great voice, and I hope you'll come use it tonight."

"You'd really let me back in the production?" Missy edged over to the table and sat down. "You'd really trust me again?"

"Everyone deserves a second chance," Lily said. "But let me down again, and I'll personally—"

"She won't," Muriel and Jack chorused.

"Now go get some sleep," Lily said to Missy. "That's an order from your director. You're not playing *Return of the Zombie*."

"How about some pie first?" Muriel suggested.

Jack sat down next to Lily as Muriel went to the counter. "I'm not saying the fight is over now," he warned her. "Just maybe postponed a week."

Lily made sparring motions with her fists. "I'm ready, Jack."

Half an hour later, her spirits high, her mouth still tingling from the sweet-tart pie, she all but skipped out of the Clarksons' house. Nothing short of an earthquake would keep Missy from playing Rosabella that night.

As she drove back to Pennyroyal Vineyards, a phrase kept echoing through Lily's mind. *Second chance*. The fates had been kind enough to give *her* a second chance, sending her Tom just when she'd begun to think she and Cleo would be going it on their own forever. And she'd been Tom's second chance, bringing love and laughter back into a life that had known too much grief. They owed it to the fates to guard their precious gift.

Maybe they'd taken too much for granted, exulting in their great good luck in finding each other, assuming luck would light their way forever. They'd always mocked other couples who went solemnly on and on about the "hard work" of marriage. They seemed to have signed a mutual, unspoken pact to avoid heavy dialogues and probing examinations of their relationship. They'd always muddled through, to use a favorite phrase of Tom's, one of them usually charming the other out of a blue mood, or both of them ignoring a problem until it went away. Even when they did have one of their awful fights, it usually ended as abruptly as it had begun. If they could be unreasonably angry with each other, they could also be unreasonably forgiving. Something always happened to remind them of their luck in having found each other.

As Lily approached Pennyroyal Vineyards, a glance at the parking lot in front of the tasting room showed that Saturday-morning business was up to standard. Given Tom's mood at the breakfast table, it was unlikely he would try to do any selling. Lily supposed she ought to spend an hour behind the counter herself, helping out Maryanne and Maureen Bailey. Personable and efficient though the twins were, they weren't magicians. They would appreciate another hand.

After parking the Datsun, she walked over to her famous vegetable garden. Tiered and densely populated according to old-fashioned theories of companion planting, the garden offered a dazzling array of colors and shapes, ranging from the delicate silvery greens of the thyme plants to the rambunctious reds of tomato plants. For absolute beauty, Lily knew her vegetable patch couldn't compete with the spectacular flower garden in front of the Navarro Vineyards tasting room in nearby Anderson Valley. But, despite her name, she had more of a feeling for vegetables than for flowers. Anyway, why look to compete at another's art when you had your own? Better to have the best-looking vegetable garden in front of a northern California winery than the second-best flower garden.

Sure that her thoughts bore some kind of moral she could apply to her life with Tom, she bent over the fragrant tomato plants, searching for aphids. If any of the little pests were afoot, they eluded her, as did the mental parallel she was looking for. She meditatively pulled up a weed that had impudently pushed through the earth next to her showiest tarragon plant. Companion planting eliminated most pests and weeds, but there were always invaders in even the most tightly controlled environments. Like Mark Davenport and Jack Clarkson invading the near-perfect precincts of her marriage.

Back up at the house, she found a blatant reminder of Mark's intrusion into the marriage. On the kitchen counter, between a bowl of green apples and a wooden box of chef's knives, stood Mark's flamboyant present: the outsize box of Night Blooming Lilies.

Picking up the box, Lily resisted the impulse to hurl it into the wastebasket. Someone would enjoy it; she had no right to waste it. As she stared at the pretty pattern on the box, she wondered if she'd spoken truthfully when she'd told Tom she would probably hate the scent now. Her curiosity mounted as she went upstairs, set the box on her dressing table, took a quick shower, and donned the ivory lace slip she would wear under her thin, translucent lavender cotton shirt dress.

Sitting at her dressing table and adding a last subtle shading of lavender to her eyelids, she finally gave in to her curiosity. Carefully she opened the box and extracted a smaller green-felt-covered box. Feeling a bit like Pandora, she opened the second box and gave a smile of recognition at the sight of the fluted glass bottle inside. Tightly stoppered, the bottle had no seal to be broken and betray her. With the bottle tight in her left hand, she turned the stopper with her right until it came free.

Cautiously she lowered her nose and inhaled. An aroma as overbearing and discordant as the cosmetics counter in a department store rose to greet her. What had once seemed the essence of sophistication now struck her senses as chemical and tawdry. The contrasting note of sweetness she'd prized seemed sickeningly cloying.

Suddenly she froze. She heard Tom's footsteps coming up the stairs. Returning to life, she hastily tried to stopper the offending bottle. But nervousness made her clumsy, and she splashed a drop of the powerful scent on her wrist. She restored the package to its pristine condition before Tom entered the room, but it seemed to her that the whole world must reek of Night Blooming Lilies.

"Hi, darling," she said heartily to Tom, as though enough vocal volume might mask the perfume, just as too-loud music could blunt the tastebuds in a restaurant. "Guess who's going to the tasting lunch with you?"

"Are you?" A look of such genuine pleasure crossed his face that Lily almost burst into tears of relief. "What happened to my steady date? Don't tell me— Gideon?"

Lily laughed, suffused with the suddenly renewed complicity between them. "Yes. First Cleo decided she shouldn't go to the lunch in case he was there and would think she was pursuing him. Then he called to announce he was going and invited her. So I'm playing second fiddle!"

"Some second fiddle." Peeling off his work clothes and bundling them under his arm, Tom headed for the bathroom. "You're first string, Wonder Woman, and you always will be." He got the shower going, then called out, "Do you forgive my grumpiness at breakfast?"

"What grumpiness?" Lily returned lightly, too enchanted with their unexpected harmony to confide her fears and anger of the morning.

"I guess it upset me that Mark made the courtly gesture I should have made after your heroic performance last night," Tom said over the sound of running water. "Not because it was Mark, or that damned perfume, but because it wasn't me."

"I seem to recall your giving me something pretty special last night," Lily said.

"There's more where it came from," Tom said, then got into the shower and closed the sliding glass door.

Lily heaved a sigh of relief. As soon as Tom came out of the shower, she would scrub her arms up to the elbow and wash away any traces of Night Blooming Lilies. "Thank you, kindly fates," she whispered, and applied her mascara with the steadiest of hands.

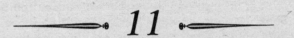

11

THEY WERE WELL past the Dromedary's Humps, almost in Haiku, when the fates revealed themselves for the tricksters they were.

Wrinkling his nose, Tom began sniffing conspicuously. "Lily," he began, in a voice that made her heart sink, "what do I smell?"

"Smell?" she echoed foolishly, trying for cheery innocence.

"Smell. *S-m-e-l-l*. As in perfume. As in Night Blooming Lilies." Pulling the car to a savage halt at the Route 101 intersection, he turned to look at her.

To her astonishment, what she saw in his eyes was not so much anger as profound sadness. "Have you been missing your old life that much?" he asked, his voice almost pitying. He put his hand under her chin in a gentle gesture, then dropped it.

"Oh, Tom." She shook her head. "What exactly

do you think I miss? The fights? The loneliness? The feeling that Cleo would never have a real father? Don't be a dope," she said tenderly.

"Then why the perfume?" Tom demanded, oblivious to the green light. "Was this your idea of how to get even with me for storming away from the breakfast table?"

"It was an accident," Lily said simply.

"An accident?"

As if underscoring the double meaning of Tom's word, a man in a yellow Porsche pulled up behind them and tooted his horn. With jerky motions, Tom made the right turn onto Route 101 and pulled into a semi-circular driveway with a dozen free spaces. "How the hell do you open a perfume bottle by accident?"

"I *opened* it quite on purpose," Lily said. "I was curious, that's all. Wouldn't you have been? It was my trademark for a long time." Her hand touched the string of pearls at her throat. "The way these are now."

"And the first whiff stirred up so many wonderful memories that you accidentally dabbed some on?" Tom's eyes glittered, daring her to call him fool enough to believe such a story.

"Oh, Tom, don't be silly," Lily said, her voice coming back to life. "I hated the smell. It all but nauseated me. I was about to close up the bottle and put it away when I heard your footsteps on the stairs. I was so nervous that my hand shook, and I ended up spilling some on myself. I scrubbed my hands after you came out of the shower, but I guess the perfume splashed on some parts I didn't scrub. In the closeness of the car, you smelled it. I'm sorry."

"Lily—"

Anger welling in her now, Lily went on, "I know there isn't time for me to go back home and shower. So why don't you drop me off at the bookstore or the movie house and go to the lunch alone? You can tell Cleo I got a headache and didn't want to drink wine. In fact, I do have a headache." Folding her arms across her chest, she stared out the car window, seeing nothing.

Tom's arm crept around her. "Lily. Look at me. Please."

Resolutely she shook her head. If she looked at him, she would lose all control; and at the moment control seemed to be all she had.

"All right, then," Tom went on, "I'll apologize to your back. It's not easy for me to say, 'I'm sorry' twice in one day, but I'll try. I'm sorry." His hand traced a tender pattern on her neck, underneath her warm hair. "I don't know what's gotten into me lately. We've had some irrigation problems up where the Gamay grapes are, and maybe I've let them get to me. Or I'm having a mid-life crisis, or some such damn thing."

His tone implied he was really immune to such crises, but Lily turned to face him anyway.

"Are you, Tom? Is this something we should talk about?"

Tom groaned. "I was joking. You know I don't believe in any of that pop psychology."

Lily put a finger to his forehead. "You don't believe you have a psyche, period. You man of iron."

"Come on, Lily. Everyone has off days. I'll snap out of this mood."

Determined this time not to let the moment for

truth get away, Lily resisted the impulse to kiss and make up. This wasn't the ideal time and place for a confrontation, but maybe such a time would never be. At least they weren't up against a deadline. Tom had kept up a good speed coming across the mountain. And, though no one did much, if any, drinking before a tasting lunch, there was always a good forty-five minutes of milling about. Anyway, better to be late for the lunch than to leave things as they stood in the Langdon marriage.

"Tom," Lily began, "is it hard for you having Mark in this part of the world? Maybe you should just accept the fact that he's thrown you off base."

Now it was Tom's turn to fold his arms across his chest. "I'm perfectly happy to admit anything that's true. But, dammit, Lily, I won't have you thinking I'm jealous of Mark. The obvious cause of a problem isn't always the true cause, you know. Anyway, I've hardly seen the man since he got here. Or felt his presence. He seems to be keeping a low profile in all our lives, for which I'm grateful. You saw us last night. Big handshake and all that. If we've got a problem—and I'm not convinced we do—you're going to have to look elsewhere for the explanation."

"If you feel so easy about Mark," Lily said softly, "explain your almost violent passion for me last night."

"Aw, honey, I did explain it. Worrying about you being too good an actress and all. And there was a full moon, don't forget. Was I really responsible for my actions?"

Lily playfully swiped at him. "Man of iron not immune to pull of moon?"

"Not immune to the pull of you." Unfastening his

seat belt, he leaned over and very gently kissed her lips. Tracing the path of her seat belt across her right breast and down to her left hip, he murmured, "So this is what bondage fantasies are all about." He pressed the release button for her belt and extricated her. "I'd rather have you free," he said, urging her into his arms.

"Tom, we're right in the middle of Haiku," Lily protested as his fingers moved suggestively over the buttons of her dress. "Which parking lot is this, anyway?" Peering out the window, she gave a sudden whoop of laughter. "Oh, good grief. The infamous Haiku Happy Rest Motel. Whatever made you pull in here?"

"Just lucky, I guess."

"Listen, I've got a great idea," Lily said, sitting up. "Let's rent a room, and I'll take a shower. Seriously. It's such bad etiquette to go to a tasting wearing perfume. The rooms here can't cost that much, and as long as I stay away from the bed, I probably won't get bitten."

Tom laughed. "Oh, Lily—"

"Isn't it a good idea?"

"Listen, Wonder Woman, I probably have a better Night Blooming Lilies detector than anyone else around Haiku. You'll do unwashed." Sniffing conspicuously, he said, "I think it's gone away."

"No, you've just gotten used to it," Lily said. "Truly. I'll be horribly self-conscious. What if someone says something in front of Cleo and Gideon? I'd be so upset. I don't want to take a chance. Give me fifteen minutes and then come back for me. Didn't you want to go into Ratchet's for something?"

Tom nodded. "A bunch of test tubes cracked in the dishwasher yesterday, and I ought to replace them." Laughing again, he said, "Okay, lady. It'll be a story to tell the grandchildren. I'll go to the office with you so I know where to find you. Anyway, in case you're seen booking a room, I want to be damned sure I'm seen with you."

"And what will you say when the manager tells you it's nice to see you back again so soon?"

Tom ruffled her hair. "You do get the strangest notions. Do you really think I've been carrying on with someone? Is that what's behind all this worrying of yours? Who's number one on your list of suspects—Muriel Clarkson? She offered to let me eat strawberry-rhubarb pie off her quivering thighs, and I couldn't resist?"

Lily met the warm gaze of his eyes, more green than brown today. "No, I really haven't worried that there was someone else," she said honestly. "But it's not just faithfulness to my body that I want; it's faithfulness to our ideas about marriage. We've been at odds too much for my comfort. That fierce intimacy seems to have vanished."

"You're rewriting history," Tom insisted as they got out of the car and started toward the manager's office. "A couple of off days and you're suddenly imagining we've had off years. I think you're the one who's been thrown by Mark's arrival—memories of a failed marriage making you wonder, maybe, if all marriages aren't fragile. This one isn't," he said, throwing an arm around her shoulders. "You've got to trust me. Most of all, you've got to trust yourself. Me man of iron. You Wonder Woman."

As they entered the motel office, he muttered, "Talk about central casting." The manager, a middle-aged man in a limp, short-sleeved white shirt and unprepossessing gray slacks, had the pale, weary eyes of someone who had seen too much of the down side of humanity.

Lily was tempted to point out that she and Tom wore matching wedding rings, but she doubted the man would be especially uplifted by the news that he had a bona fide married couple signing his register. He merely pointed to each blank that had to be filled in—name, address, make of car, and license plate.

"That's eight-fifty," he said, scanning the register with uninterested eyes. "In advance."

"I've got it," Tom said, reaching for his wallet.

"Oh, no. This one's on me," Lily couldn't resist saying, opening her purse.

"Shall we split it?" Tom suggested, extracting four singles from his billfold and fishing in his pocket for a quarter.

As Lily matched him, she added mischievously, "Don't forget, you need money for the hardware store."

The motel clerk finally condescended to raise an eyebrow, then quickly reassumed his bland expression. Biting back giggles, Lily swung her key and led Tom out of the office and toward unit nine.

"Let me look the place over," Tom said as Lily unlocked the door. Camping—but somehow serious, too—he checked under the bed and in the bathroom. "Not so bad," he pronounced. "One of those reassuring paper strips across the toilet, and nothing moving in the shower. I wouldn't use the drinking glasses, though. They look a little smudgy. Let's see about the soap—oh, good. Your very own untouched thumbnail-size Cashmere Bouquet. Just about enough to do the job. Shall I stay and scrub your back?"

"I don't think I managed to splash any Night Blooming Lilies on my back." Lily started to unbutton her dress. "Gads, what a place," she said, taking in the suggestive pink walls, the badly reproduced Impressionist nude in a metal frame, and a large mirror artfully placed just opposite the bed. "Do you think anyone ever comes here to sleep?"

"They probably have different rooms for more respectable people," Tom teased. "With landscapes on the wall. But the manager took one look at us and thought: Ah, unit nine." He caught his breath as Lily stepped out of her dress, displaying a lacy length of ivory slip. "Isn't it amazing? I saw you in that slip— what, an hour ago? But seeing you take off your dress just now did something to me."

"And then of course the magnificent ambience," Lily said, tossing back her hair, warming under Tom's liquid stare. "Well, if you're going to Ratchet's, shouldn't you go? We don't want to be late." To her chagrin, the words seemed to jumble in her throat. She put a hand to the strap of her slip, then stood unmoving, waiting.

"I was thinking," Tom said, "that maybe I should have a shower, too."

"Oh? In case any Night Blooming Lilies rubbed off on you?"

"Exactly," he said. "Exactly. Do you mind sharing the facilities? There are two bars of soap, I noticed. Towels aplenty."

"I'd be happy to," Lily murmured. "We can't have

you offending all those educated noses, can we?" She took off her slip, revealing sheer ivory bikini panties and a matching bra that offered up her soft skin rather than concealing it.

In an instant Tom had stripped to the red and navy European-cut briefs Lily had bought in San Francisco to jazz up his underwear wardrobe.

"Your best panties, I see." She made an approximation of a lewd wink. "Did you plan this event?" she asked suspiciously.

"My mother told me always to be prepared. And men don't wear panties, by the way. These are briefs. Repeat after me."

"Panties." Lily stuck out her tongue.

"You're very fresh, young woman, you know that? You know what happens to fresh young women?"

"I'm not afraid. I know you didn't get to the hardware store." Lily giggled.

Tom looked sorrowfully down at his underwear. "I suppose there's nothing to do, then, but take them off. The consequences may be more than you reckoned on."

As he stripped, Lily let out a low whistle of appreciation. "And what do you call that?" she asked pertly, clasping her hands behind her, letting her eyes do the caressing.

"I call it Little Johnny Jump-Up, my dear. Want to pet it? It won't bite."

"I don't know, mister. I just came here for a shower." Pretending alarm, Lily fled to the bathroom, turned on the shower, and took off her bra and panties.

"Ahah." Tom came in just as she was unwrapping a miniature cake of soap. "So this is where you fled to. There's no escaping me now, my girl." Opening his own soap, he followed Lily into the shower-tub, pulling the frosted glass door snugly closed.

"Woman," Lily said defiantly. "I'm not a girl."

"Woman, are you? We'll see about that." As the water splashed merrily over her breasts and trickled down her flat belly, Tom traced spirals over the path with his soap. "I have to admit, you feel sort of womanly. Turn around, though. I'm not through checking."

As Lily faced the other way, averting her head to keep the spray from her makeup and hair, Tom lathered her hips and buttocks. "A woman, all right," he murmured. "Have to admit it."

Pressing against her from behind, encircling her breasts with his arms, he let her feminine curves feel his maleness. He turned her slightly so she had a tile wall to lean against. "And what a woman." His soapy hands slid everywhere, pressing home the message of his passion. "What a glorious woman."

Lily closed her eyes, giving herself up to sensation. The sharp pelting of the water contrasted gorgeously with the round, silky motions Tom's hands were making. Inside the closed-up bath, her world had never seemed smaller or more exquisite. The noise of the shower was a private music screening out all external reality. She and Tom were the beginning and the end of time, all the men and women who ever had been and ever would be.

He began kissing her hair, his lips lazily etching a path toward her ear. Feeling weightless, she spun around in his arms, offering her cheeks, chin, nose, and lips up to his kisses. Their probing tongues danced around each other, giving and demanding at once.

Reluctantly pulling free of the torrid embrace, Lily said throatily, "It's my turn to wash you." Soap in hand, she drew a heart on his chest, then filled it in with her initials. Laughing tenderly at the strangely innocent sight of his lathered chest hair, she sketched vines and leaves, finally drawing a fig leaf or two where a naked man might most want it.

How precious he felt in her hands! As she manipulated him toward the stream of water, rinsing off every trace of soap, she was struck by the enormous amount of trust conveyed in every naked encounter. She had no doubt that she deserved Tom's trust; she cherished his skin as she did her own. She knew she was just as safe in his hands. If he had his moments of near roughness, she had to admit she wanted such moments. His roughness was just another version of his tenderness, a different way of branding the same message into her body: I love you, I want you.

Urged on by the pounding yet soothing water warming her skin, Lily knelt, drinking droplets off Tom's thighs. As her mouth moved upward, her tongue darting everywhere, she felt him begin to tremble.

"Lord, Lily, is this why more accidents happen in bathtubs than—" His words gave way to a sound of intoxicated pleasure; his hands went to her hair, holding her, guiding her. "Is this really happening? I've died and gone to heaven. More. Stop. Oh, Lily, you're the most magical creature who ever lived." Suddenly he tugged her to her feet. "I have to have you. Totally. Now."

"Here? We'll drown. But what a way to go," she murmured into his chest. Her words spiraled into a squeal as the water pressure suddenly dropped and the water temperature plummeted.

Shielding her from the icy spray, Tom reached for the control dial and turned off the shower. He grabbed a towel and briskly began rubbing her dry.

Recovering from her shock, she burst into peals of laughter.

"Not so funny," Tom said ruefully, toweling himself. "You know what cold showers are always prescribed for."

"You mean that's the end?"

"Well, not forever," he said. "If you'll just give me your telephone number..."

Lily looked wistfully at the bed. "It has a Magic Fingers vibrator and everything."

"I'm out of quarters, anyway," Tom said. "I gave at the office." Pulling Lily to him, he added, "We can always come back. I never would have dreamed you'd find the Haiku Happy Rest Motel so stirring. We could have saved a fortune on our vacations if I'd known you had this tacky side. I always figured I had to put you in deluxe accommodations or not get any action."

"You keep that illusion," Lily said into his chest. Sighing, she added, "I suppose we should get dressed, and go to that lunch."

"From the divine to the lunch," Tom said. He brushed Lily's lips with his own. "I do love you, Lily mine. Here, there, everywhere. We have a good time, don't we?"

She reached for her bra and panties. "We have a

fantastic time." Hesitating for an instant, she had to add, "And sometimes an awful time. If our best wasn't so good, I guess I wouldn't mind our fights so much. But I do. They're such nightmares for me."

"Except that we always come back to our sweet dream state. And always will. You know that, don't you?"

"Sometimes it's hard to have faith," she said. She looked into the mirror as she fastened her pearls around her neck. The shower had given her hair extra wave, but she bore no other marks of the sublime last half hour. "You seem so different when we fight. So— not there."

"We're two strong-willed people," Tom said as he stepped into his briefs. "Equals. That's why we fight so hard. Give me another seven years, and I'll have you enjoying our arguments."

"Don't make it your top priority."

He shook his head. "Absolutely not. Top priority is coming back here with you and a sack full of quarters. Good heaven, it's almost one o'clock. May I borrow a comb?"

12

LILY'S PENCIL HOVERED over her wine-evaluation sheet. Their host for the lunch, young Peter Esterhazy, had filled four glasses for each person present, pouring from bottles that he'd elaborately disguised with napkins. Now his thirty or so guests were supposed to evaluate each wine on a scale of zero to two points according to appearance, color, aroma, acid, sugar, body, flavor, and general quality. The tasters would then total their points and rank the wines in order of preference.

First taking a bite of unbuttered bread to clear her palate, Lily sipped from the glass to her far left, a translucent white wine with desirable hints of green and gold in color. Her nose caught a rather heavy whiff of raisin, but the taste eluded her completely. All she could taste was Tom—soapy Tom, water-washed Tom, aroused Tom. She looked across the table to see if he was having similar trouble, but his pencil was flying down his sheet as he made his notations with imperious certainty. At the next table, Cleo and Gideon were evincing the same kind of certainty. Lily noticed with amusement that they were shielding their evaluation sheets from each other, like college sweethearts wanting to be sure that the proctor couldn't accuse them of cheating on their exam.

Lily took another sip of the elusive wine. There was definitely some raisin in the taste, too much for her liking. Although the sugar and acid seemed nicely balanced, the sensation left in her mouth after she'd swallowed—the finish, as it was known in the tasting game—reminded her of the raisin cookies she'd hated as a kid, the sort that looked as though they had squashed bugs in them.

The sound of a suppressed giggle from Cleo's direction made her look up again. Something about the body language of Cleo and Gideon conveyed to Lily that a knee had just nudged a knee or a foot had made overtures to an ankle. Whatever the connection was, it was making them both blush with pleasure. And creating a quiet stir among the gathered grape growers and winemakers. Gideon was the first Alexander to participate in a tasting lunch or any other Haiku area oenological activity. His parents had always operated in grand isolation from their thick-walled chateau, sending a clear message to the rest of Haiku Valley and nearby wine-growing enclaves that they were too big, too good to need the advice of the local winemaking fraternity.

With a sudden flash of intuition, Lily took a bite

of bread to chase the taste of wine number three (a pale, excessively acidic blend), then went back to the first glass. Yes, she was sure of it. This was the much ballyhooed Alexander Cellars Chardonnay of two years past. Much ballyhooed by the Alexanders and their publicists, that is, but severely taken to task by Tom and other local savants as a rather vulgar wine, made for the know-nothing status seekers and vastly overpriced to give it a cachet it didn't earn on its merits.

Lily covertly eyed her host, sitting on her left. Had Peter Esterhazy invited Gideon to the tasting in hopes of embarrassing him? Peter was just about Gideon's age and stood to inherit nearly as much fertile land; someday the two young men would be the two lords of Haiku Valley. She'd always thought of Peter as nice, if colorless—too nice to set out to embarrass someone. But the Alexander elders had snubbed him time and again, giving him no more consideration than they gave to old Dicky Planchard, with his hand-drawn labels, funky little tasting room, and an annual production of a mere five hundred cases.

After ranking the other three wines, eating a bite of bread, and swallowing some water, Lily went back to the first wine yet again. As she lifted it to her lips, Tom gave her a long wink, confirming her conviction that it was the Alexander Chardonnay. Her heart sank for Gideon as she thought of how Tom and some of his confreres would rate the wine—fourth, probably; third at best. And if Gideon felt humiliated, heaven only knew what it would do to his nascent relationship with Cleo. Lily still wasn't sure how she felt about the relationship, but she didn't want it subjected to some ridiculous external pressure. If a seven-year-old marriage could be rocked by the likes of a letter from Jack Clarkson in the *Herald,* a day-old infatuation might well be detonated by a public humiliation.

Emitting a stagy "Hmm," and calling on her acting skills to convey the idea that she'd suddenly had a genuine change of mind, Lily began erasing the zeros and ones she'd put in the column under wine number one, replacing them with twos. Adding the new figures, that wine had a total of fourteen points, nosing out the fourth wine as her favorite.

Now, if only she had some way of tipping off Cleo to the identity of that wine! Or had Cleo, with her evermore discerning palate, realized what she was drinking? Lily ransacked her memory, going back to the night that Tom had brought home a bottle of the expensive, much-promoted Alexander Cellars Chardonnay. Had Cleo been home for dinner that night? Or had she been off at a movie with friends? The details were vague, but Lily was pretty sure she and Tom had consumed the bottle themselves, ending up making sweet, sleepy, very married love.

Anyway, even if she could find a way to let Cleo know it was Alexander Cellars wine, Lily wasn't sure Cleo would change her vote. In the time-honored tradition of teenagers, Cleo tended to see things as black or white. Truth was truth, dishonesty was dishonesty, never mind the gray areas in between. Lily would just have to make her own gesture, and hope for the best.

"Mind all made up?" asked the man on her left, Leonard Fitch, a Chicago stockbroker who'd bought a hundred acres outside Haiku and planted them with champagne grapes.

"Pretty much," Lily said. "Though I'm never sure

that on any given day I wouldn't vote totally differently."

"I know what you mean," said the balding, portly
Leonard. "I'm just glad it's not a Champagne tasting.
Not that I have a vintage ready for tasting yet, but I
think I'd be nervous anyway."

A waiter set glass bowls of celery, olives, and
radishes on the table, the vegetables glistening under
a sprinkling of crushed ice. Lily made a face at the
banal offering. Each item in the bowl had its honorable
place in cuisine, but radishes needed butter, black
bread, salt, and iced vodka to complement their pun-
gency; celery lost most of its flavor if allowed to soak
in ice water, as this batch clearly had done; and those
olives were the bland, tinned variety, not the pungent
and meaty spiced, brined olives Lily loved.

She took a stalk of celery, anyway.

"Not quite up to your pre-theater buffets," Leonard
said softly, not wanting to be rude to their host. Even
though each "guest" paid ten dollars for the meal, it
was up to the host to pick the restaurant and the menu.
In this instance, the restaurant was A la Bonne Femme,
a half-timbered Tudor on the outside, with heavy
paneling and numerous fireplaces on the inside, and
a kitchen heavily committed to sauces and elaborate
garnishes.

"Were you at the theater last night?" Lily asked.
"I didn't see you—but, then, I didn't see much."

"I heard all about your gallant performance," Leonard said with as much of a bow as a seated man could
manage, "and I wish I'd been there. I have tickets for
Wednesday night. To tell you the truth, I'm one of
those crabby people who can't bear musical comedies.

But after reading that ridiculous letter in the *Herald*, I got on the phone and ordered two tickets. I know I'll enjoy the food, anyway."

Lily impulsively bent over and kissed him on the cheek. "Bless you. Maybe the show will surprise you. We really have an exceptionally good cast this time around."

"No doubt, no doubt. Will you pass the olives, please?" Picking the plumpest olive from its nest of ice, he said, "What is this ANVIL nonsense, anyway? I never heard of it before yesterday."

"It didn't exist before yesterday," spoke up a tanned blonde sitting on Tom's left. "And I doubt it will ever exist anywhere but in Jack Clarkson and Buck Olly's minds. Meanwhile, the backlash is terrific for business." The blonde was named Pamela Venable and owned, with her husband, the other tasting room that Jack had singled out because it featured new music. "Poor Jack," she went on. "Male menopause, or something. I bet he wishes he'd never written the silly thing."

Lily noted that Tom was listening impassively to the conversation. Would he try telling Pamela what he'd told her—that Jack deserved to be taken seriously? Or had he changed his own tune?

She wasn't going to find out at the moment. Peter Esterhazy was rapping his fork against his water glass for attention and rising to his feet.

"Judging by the haste with which the olives and celery are being consumed, we have a hungry crowd," he said. "So I thought we'd tabulate our tasting results and get on with some serious eating and drinking."

Responding to the scattered applause, he said, "Are you ready, Eileen?"

"Ready," said his dark-haired, petite wife, getting to her feet at another table and positioning her pencil at her clipboard. "We won't reveal the labels until after the votes are in, but we'll let you know this much now. All the wines we tasted today are two-year-old Chardonnays. They vary in price from seven dollars the bottle to eighteen. Different as they are, each one has taken a silver or gold medal at a California fair." Allowing time for a murmur of appreciation to ripple around the tables, Eileen Esterhazy went on, "Now let's have some rankings."

Lily nervously listened to the tabulations. Although the guests seemed widely to disagree as to the first, second, and third place wines, a decided majority were declaring wine number one—the Alexander Cellars Chardonnay—their fourth-place choice. Stealing a look at Gideon and Cleo, she saw only impassive faces. Poor Gideon! Then Lily heard Tom start to speak, and she gave him all her attention.

"My first choice is wine number one," her disbelieving ears heard. "Then come two, four, and three," Tom said, "in that order." An expectant expression on his face, he listened as the others around the table gave their rankings. Three guests put the Alexander wine last, and one rated it third.

"One, four, two, three," Lily said simply when her turn came. Scarcely daring to look at Tom, she was gratified to feel his foot nudge hers under the table. That clinched it! He knew why she'd rigged her rankings, and he'd rigged his for the same reason. Good-heartedness and love for Cleo was what it came down to. She almost wanted to cry.

The surprises weren't over yet. Cleo unhesitatingly rated the Alexander wine as third. And Gideon ranked it fourth!

Standing up, the sleek-haired, slender young man said, "Lest anyone here think that two years away has addled my brains, let me tell you that I'm certain that fourth-place wine is none other than the famed Alexander Cellars Chardonnay. Right, Peter and Eileen?"

Reddening, his hosts acknowledged the fact.

"I'm proud," Gideon went on, "of many of the wines my parents have made. But this particular vintage was blended, priced—overpriced, I daresay—and marketed under the supervision of a group of people who have no future at Alexander Cellars. My father has asked me to be his winemaker and to overhaul some other areas of the business, including public relations. So this is a warning," he went on lightly. "If there's an Alexander Chardonnay in a blind tasting two years from now, you're all going to end up ranking it first—even if your own wines are on the table."

Laughter and applause rang out in the room. Peter Esterhazy crossed to Gideon's table to offer him his hand.

"I didn't believe you'd come to the tasting," Lily heard Peter say. "No Alexander ever has. I hope you don't think—"

"No problem, Peter," Gideon said lightly.

After the lunch, a more palatable meal than Lily had expected, ending with a truly superb frozen hazelnut cake, Gideon headed straight for Lily and Tom.

"Thank you," he said simply. "I know why you voted the way you did."

Tom shrugged lightly. "The mysteries of taste."

"I like to think I'd have done the same sort of thing if I felt someone was being put at a disadvantage," Gideon went on.

"Frankly," Tom said, "I don't think anyone could ever put you at a disadvantage."

"Is that a compliment?" Gideon asked.

"It's a fact," Tom said simply, clapping the younger man on the shoulder and walking away.

"Well, you've certainly grown up, young Gideon," Lily said.

"Mostly last night," he replied.

"Oh?" Lily's maternal heart began pounding.

"After five minutes with Cleo, I realized how corrupt my taste in women had become in Europe. I may have learned a lot about being a winemaker over there, but I'm not sure I learned a lot about being a human being."

"And now you know it all?"

"I know what I have to learn," he answered solemnly. "And I know who I want to be my teacher."

"That sounds pretty serious," Lily commented.

"Because it is pretty serious. And I think my feelings are reciprocated."

Lily looked across the room. Cleo's eyes were shining. Her movements and posture had an enchanting giddiness to them. She was very obviously smitten.

"I hate to sound like somebody's mother," Lily said, "but you two have known each other for less than twenty-four hours."

"We were friends before I left for France," Gideon said. He smiled, lighting up a dimple on the left side of his mouth and looking very young and dear.

"We're not talking just friends, are we?" Lily asked.

Gideon's nostrils flared. "No, we're not. We're talking anything's possible. Anything and everything. In time."

"You mean you'll wait another day before you get *really* serious?" Lily teased.

"How long did it take you and Tom?" Gideon asked bluntly.

"About thirty seconds," she replied. Taking in Gideon's wide, reddish eyebrows, his impeccably shaved chin, the crisp yet casual red and white striped oxford-cloth shirt with rolled up sleeves, she had no trouble seeing his outward allure. And he'd shown himself to be a man of character today, making his own stand in the world without being disloyal to his parents. But he was so young! And Cleo was a baby. "Tom and I were older," she went on. "We'd both been through a lot. We each had a child and a marriage behind us. You could say we'd done a lot of groundwork before it got to those thirty seconds."

Cleo came sauntering over then and casually linked her arm through Gideon's. "He's nice, isn't he?" she asked her mother, exhibiting a brand-new self-possession.

"Very," Lily agreed. "Cute, too."

Gideon flashed his dimple again, but he didn't blush. All right, Lily thought, so he knew he was cute. Tom had always known, too.

"And you think we're crazy to be so sure of each other, don't you?" Cleo said.

"Very," Lily repeated.

"Don't worry, Mama," Cleo said, using a nomenclature she'd retired years ago. "We're only rushing in our minds."

"That's good to know," Lily said soberly. Hugging Cleo then Gideon, she said, "It's wonderful for me that you've been so open. I'm still in a state of shock, but you've kept it from being fatal."

Gideon and Cleo started making the rounds of the room. Lily ran to pry Tom away from a conversation with Leonard Fitch about pest control.

"Tom," she said, "can we head for home? We've got to talk."

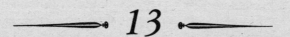

13

THEY WERE ON the far side of the Dromedary's Humps before Lily's monologue ran out of steam and Tom was able to get in a word. "She's eighteen. She's not a baby," he said.

"But she's been so protected," Lily protested, slumping back into her seat.

"Protected? This child who flies off to New York to visit her father, who's grown up in the city and country, the East Coast and West Coast?"

"Oh, sophisticated in a way," Lily agreed. "But protected from the world of sex, somehow. What scares me, Tom, is that only yesterday she was talking about how much she wanted a man who would love her as a woman. A man," she added after a moment of hesitation, "who would love her the way you love me."

Tom took his eyes off the road for a moment to

look quizzically at Lily. "Did she really? How touching. And you held out on me."

"We were fighting," Lily conceded. "I couldn't make you feel too good, right?" Patting his thigh, she said soothingly, "I had it filed away for a moment when you needed reassurance. If such a moment ever came. Anyway," she went on, not really wanting to be deflected, "one minute this wish was in Cleo's mind, and then along came Gideon. Isn't that timing too good to believe?"

"You mean you think she's reading qualities into him he doesn't possess?" Tom hugged the inside of the mountain as a truck came lumbering by from the other direction. "You okay, babe?" he asked, feeling Lily's shudder.

"Fine," she said weakly. "I'm going to have to get used to this road if we start commuting to the Haiku Happy Rest Motel."

"Give me another seven years—" Tom began cheerfully.

Lily sighed volubly. "That's what I wish we could give Cleo. Or get her to give herself. Time."

"Look," Tom said, "I'm not so sure they're in such a hurry to do anything concrete. Become lovers, for instance. Or get married. I think for various reasons they just felt an urge to declare themselves to us. Maybe Gideon needs to tell the world he's serious about Haiku Valley. And what better way than by linking himself with the loveliest young woman in the area? Francesca or one of his friends may have told him that rumors floated back here about his involvement with—what was she—that French baroness? And, just to take a stab in the dark, maybe Cleo has felt some of the tension we've been having lately and wanted to dissociate herself from it."

"So you admit we've been having tension." Lily pounced on the idea.

"I never denied it," Tom said. "I just refuse to take it seriously."

"But we don't agree about anything anymore," Lily wailed. "It seems the last straw to disagree about something concerning Cleo."

"Dammit, Lily, what do you mean, 'the last straw'? Didn't we just have a fabulous romp? And didn't we both do something at the tasting lunch that made us feel wonderfully in accord? You seem determined to see our relationship in the darkest possible light."

"And you seem determined to see it through a rosy glow," Lily returned.

Silence prevailed until they reached Pennyroyal Vineyards.

"So the upshot is that you won't say anything to Cleo?" Lily demanded as they headed up the driveway.

"Oh, Lily." Tom heaved a great sigh. "And if I did say something? Your parents said plenty to you when you fell in love with Mark at the same age. All their words did was to drive you into marriage the quicker, just to prove how grown-up you were, and how right. Why don't we just keep an eye on the young couple? For all we know, it'll end as abruptly as it began. Let's not waste our clout."

For some reason the reference to Mark incensed Lily. Before she could stop them, ugly words came rolling off her tongue. "If Cleo were really your daughter, I bet you'd feel differently."

Tom turned off the ignition with a snap so vehement that he nearly broke the key. "How dare you say that to me?" he stormed at Lily. He grabbed her shoulders, forcing her to face him. "Are you just hell-bent on making serious trouble between us? Well, you may finally have succeeded." Unsnapping his seat belt, he lunged out of the car and slammed the door behind him.

Lily covered her face with her hands. Hot tears trickled between her fingers. She'd been wrong, dead wrong, to say what she'd said. Never once before in the seven years of the marriage had either she or Tom accused each other of being less than real parents to their stepchildren. Did Tom understand that if she could rewrite history, he would be Cleo's father, her real and only father? Oh, why hadn't she met him when they were both young and free? That was what her words had really meant.

She sat there feeling sorry for herself for a moment or two, then took a tissue from her bag and wiped her eyes. She had to find Tom and make him understand that behind her bitter, ill-worded question had been a profound longing for the impossible. A very foolish longing, to be sure, but one that was in every way a compliment to him.

She made herself take a few deep breaths. In truth, she knew she should be grateful for reality as it was. She didn't really wish Cleo were different, or that Tibs were; and she couldn't rewrite history, even in her most private mind, and not change the children. All that mattered was that the four of them had one another now. She had to let Tom know that was how she felt.

She had no idea whether he had headed for the house, the tasting room, the winery, or the fields, but the house seemed the likely choice. Anyway, she wanted to splash cold water on her face.

"Tom?" she called as she walked into the kitchen. No answer. Grateful for a few moments of solitude to compose herself, she wondered where Tibs was. A note scrawled in red ink and left weighted down next to the kitchen telephone caught her eye and provided the answer.

Dear Dad & Lily—
    Mark called from the inn—has terminal cabin fever. I'm off to rescue him. Will probably take him up to Mendocino for lunch. Home around three-thirty, four.
    Missy Clarkson called. Said she'll be in the green room at seven. (Good work, Step-Ma!)
    Buck Olly called for Dad. Sounded nervous. Maryanne said tasting room may set a record today. Some guy from Philadelphia wants every bottle of Gewurtz. you have! Am impressed!
                Love,
                Tibs

What a sweetheart of a boy, Lily thought—and flinched. She loved him absolutely, which was how Tom loved Cleo. She would feel wounded to the core if her love for Tibs had been impugned.

Cold water helped alleviate the redness in her eyes but inspired no perfect act of contrition. She would just have to find Tom and let her heart speak.

As she was descending the stairs, she heard the

screen door to the kitchen bang. "Tom?" she called out, her voice breathless.

"Tibs," came back merrily. "And Mark."

Lily swallowed a groan. Of all times to have to deal with Mark! But there was nothing to do save keep on going and play her part.

"Hi, there," she said cheerfully, walking into the kitchen. "Did you two do the grand tour?"

"I have seen Mendocino," Mark said resonantly. "I have done Mendocino. Mendocino did me."

"We had lunch at the Broken Croissant," Tibs said, "and they wouldn't take a credit card or Mark's check." Shrugging, he added, "All actors have to wash dishes sooner or later, right?"

"You didn't!" Lily gasped.

"Of course we didn't," Mark boomed. "This young man is enough of a personage locally so his check was taken."

Lily laughed. "Oh, Mark. Is it unbearable being someplace where you're not instantly recognized by every maître d'? Never mind. You probably had a pretty good lunch. Did you drink some Navarro Blanc de Noir? They've cornered the market on it. It's my favorite non-Pennyroyal wine." She sat down at the kitchen table and gestured at Mark and Tibs. In a moment she would excuse herself and go off in search of Tom, but meanwhile she couldn't very well be rude and leave her ex-husband and stepson just standing there.

To her dismay, Mark pulled out the chair across from her and settled into it with his actor's fluid grace, even though Tibs had announced that he was off to the tasting room to help Maureen and Maryanne. But

Tibs had already given up a chunk of his day for Mark; it wasn't fair to ask more of him. Besides, it sounded as though all hands were needed in the winery.

"I may come down later to help out, too," Lily said, paving the way to get free of Mark. Every moment that passed before she could seek peace with Tom would make it that much harder to heal the breach.

"So, my night-blooming Lily," Mark said when they were alone. "This is what it's all about." Gesturing narrowly, he seemed to be implying that the kitchen limits defined the boundaries of Lily's world. He ran his fingers through his mahagony hair and gave her a challenging look.

"Pretty grand, isn't it?" she said warmly, as if agreeing with a generous review on his part.

"Cute," he said. He put his feet against the rung of Lily's chair, showing off his Italian loafers, the same burnished mahagony as his hair. "Cute house, cute theater, cute coastline, cute family. But I never thought cuteness was what you were about."

"It never was, and it isn't now." Lily felt her face and voice shutting down, and she didn't care.

"You mean you've thought about wanting out? Getting back to the big time?"

"Oh, Mark, give it a rest, will you? This is the big time for me. The biggest time I ever hoped for." Closing her eyes for a second, she cast up a small prayer that she hadn't damaged it with her wild words to Tom. "I've never been happier."

Mark's shoulders seemed to sag. "I'm glad for you, Lily. I really am. But I have to admit it's not what I'd hoped to hear. Maybe I've read too many corny scripts lately. I couldn't help hoping on the plane out here that somehow I'd end up bringing you and Cleo back home to New York."

"I can't believe it's what you want in your deepest heart," she said gently. "I know I've changed in the years we've been apart, but not all that much. I don't expect I'd be any more of an ideal companion for you today than I was when we were together."

"When we were *married*," Mark said. "When you were my *wife*, not my companion." He reached for her hand. "We don't have much of a present, and you've made it clear we have less of a future, but won't you at least give me the past? It wasn't all misery, you know. I was happy for a while, exceedingly happy, and I think you were, too. We were in love, Lily, both of us. Tell me you remember."

She looked at him pleadingly, but he didn't relent. "I can still see you the way you looked on our wedding day," he said softly. "Much too beautiful for City Hall in that blue velvet dress."

"And you wore that pinstripe suit," she chimed in. "After teasing me that you were going to show up in jeans."

"I thought I'd die of happiness that day." Mark's mouth trembled, and he looked away. "All the theater kids toasting us at Sardi's, and then home to our very own Greenwich Village dump."

Lily laughed. "It was like playing house, wasn't it? Everything so enchanted. Even going to the supermarket was poetic." Squeezing his hand, she said, "Oh, Mark, I did love you. Not wisely, but truly."

Hearing her own words, she grew light-headed. But it wasn't a dizzy feeling so much as the kind of emptiness that comes after a much-needed emotional house-cleaning.

"Thank you," Mark said, his raspy voice gentle.

"Thank *you*," she said. "I told Cleo she was born of love, but there was still a lot of feeling I wouldn't admit to myself. Or you. I'm so glad I did."

"Tom is one lucky man." Mark touched Lily's wedding ring, then quickly withdrew his hand, as if knowing it didn't belong there.

"I'm the one who's lucky. To have had you and to have him."

"I still care for you," Mark said.

"And I for you. I do want you to be happy. Is there . . . anyone?"

"Lots of 'em," Mark said cheerfully. "But even when I douse them in Night Blooming Lilies, the magic isn't there."

"It will be," Lily said with conviction. "Maybe this trip will prove to be a watershed for us both. You're getting your proper co-star back tonight," she went on, needing a little breathing space. "I hope you'll give her as much help as you gave me last night."

"It wasn't just me. That's some good cast you have there. I have to admit, it's a pretty nifty little theater all around. Aw, hell, strike the 'little.' And while we're passing out the kudos, I suppose I should tell you what a terrific mother I think you've been. Cleo's everything I'd hoped she would be."

"Even though she's throwing away her life on wine?" Lily couldn't resist saying.

"Ouch. She and Gideon opened my eyes last night. I happily admit that. Before I leave, I'm ordering a case or two of that Gewurtztraminer from the tasting room. I like the spice, and it has a marvelous finish."

Lily laughed. "You're something else, Mark Davenport. We'll give you the family discount. What did you think of Gideon, by the way?"

"I think it's interesting how much he looks like me."

Lily glanced up in surprise. She couldn't deny the resemblance. Same slender build, very nearly the same hair, though Gideon's coloring was all his own. Interesting, really. Gideon was physically akin to one of Cleo's fathers and seemed to be akin to the other in character. Did that make her sudden commitment more reasonable, or more scary? Both, maybe. It certainly made the commitment harder to dismiss.

"Yes, he does look rather like you," Lily said. "Leaving aside the famous Davenport twice-broken nose. Oh, Mark," she burst out, "it's frightening for me. They really only met last night, and they're so serious about each other."

"These are fast times, Lily," Mark said, patting her hand.

"Never mind the times. We're talking about Cleo. Somehow I guess I imagined her going off to college with nothing on her mind but her studies and being open to the world."

"You mean you wanted her to have her heart broken a dozen times before finding the love of her life? Maybe you should be glad she might be spared that." Eyes narrowing, Mark added, "I think Tom has made something of a conservative of you."

"Don't be silly. He feels the way you apparently do. What will be, will be. But he doesn't know what it's like to live through a divorce." She wearily rested her face on her hands. Oh, where was the cushiony comfort of her kitchen now?

"Lily, Lily." Mark's voice was gentle. "You're not Cleo, and Cleo isn't you. You look a lot alike, but she isn't your clone. Just because she's fallen in love at the age you fell in love with me doesn't mean she's doomed to see the relationship fall apart. Anyway, who's rushing, you or Cleo? You're already plotting her divorce, and she hasn't even planned her wedding yet. I know empathy is the actor's stock in trade, but you're overdoing it."

Mark rose to his feet. "You look as though you could use some time on your own. If you'll call a cab for me, I'll head back to the inn. I picked up a couple of good mysteries in Mendocino, just right for reading in the hot tub."

"Cab!" Lily smiled indulgently. "I could more easily rent you a horse to ride. I'll run you home. Where are your books? In Tibs's car?"

"Along with a shawl I picked up for Cleo. Does she like shawls?" he asked anxiously.

"Exactly her sort of thing," Lily assured him.

"Speaking of which—" Mark vigorously sniffed. "I don't smell any Night Blooming Lilies."

"Oh, Mark, it was a very sweet idea, but I don't wear perfume anymore. Half of wine is in the aroma, you see, so vintners resent anything that interferes with the sense of smell. I'm afraid heady perfumes are number one on the hit list."

"So Cleo won't wear it, either," he said a bit wistfully.

"I'm afraid not." Impulsively Lily added, "Do you

want to hear what a silly, sentimental thing I am? I opened the bottle just to smell it."

"Did you?" Mark looked inordinantly pleased.

"But I didn't break a seal or mess up the box," Lily went on, "so if you possibly know another worthy recipient . . . I'll go upstairs and get the perfume and then I'll take you home. Tibs always leaves his keys in his car."

"Lily—" Mark reached out and stopped her. "You're not sorry we happened, are you?"

"Of course not," she said genuinely.

"Just because of Cleo?" Mark persisted.

"Because of everything," she said sincerely. "If I hadn't been there then, I couldn't be here now. How's that for a California answer?"

Not waiting for his reply, she dashed up the stairs.

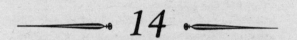

14

TOOLING ALONG ROUTE 128 after dropping off Mark, Lily felt an exhilarating sense of freedom. Part of the credit went to Tibs's sporty red Camaro. More went to the words she'd exchanged with Mark. In acknowledging what he'd been in her past, she'd somehow banished him from her present. No, not banished him, exactly; she'd just found a way of seeing him in perspective. He was real now, and life-size, not gigantic in the way of all myths, be they good or bad.

She was actually glad he was here, now. Or would be glad if Tom could straighten out his own feelings about Mark. If she and Tom could just straighten out their own feelings about every sensitive area, how very wonderful life would be again.

Though she still had to face Tom's possible coldness when she delivered her apology for the words about Cleo, she was no longer as scared as she had been. She was one step closer to the clearing.

As she turned into the driveway, the green Datsun turned in from the opposite direction. Without looking at each other, she and Tom drove up the hill in parallel formation and parked side by side. Holding her breath, she wondered if he would come to her if she remained behind the wheel. But she owed it to him to make a move, she reminded herself. She got out of the car.

He got out of his car. "Lily—" he began.

"Tom—" she began.

They stood in the driveway looking at each other.

"We have to talk," he said neutrally, has face giving away nothing.

"Yes," she agreed. "In the kitchen? It's almost time for tea."

"Tea can wait a few minutes. Let's go upstairs to our room. I don't want to take any chance on being interrupted."

Because he had such shockingly ominous things to say to her? Trembling inside, she preceded him up the stairs.

She sat down on the long wooden settee opposite the bed. Looking around the room, she tried to take comfort in the dear familiar shapes and textures. Tom was at the dormer window, looking out, his hands jammed into the pockets of his jeans. The dearest, most familiar shape of all . . .

"I've never been much good at apologizing," he began roughly, not looking at her, "but I seem to owe you one."

"You owe me? But—"

"Please, let me finish," he said. "This is hard enough

as it is." Staring out the window, he went on, "Buck Olly called. I don't know if you saw Tibs's note. I called him back, and he let me have an earful."

"You mean about how I'm destroying the valley?" Lily couldn't help saying.

Tom laughed harshly. "Hardly. About how Jack Clarkson's letter was destroying Buck's Valley Store because it mentioned that Buck was part of this ANVIL nonsense."

At the word "nonsense," Lily's heart did a jig. "Oh," she said softly.

"It seems," Tom went on, "that people have been staying away from Buck's store in droves. Staying away from Jack's wayside stand, too. And the people who have showed up have made it very clear that you're about the last person on earth they want to make trouble for." He turned and faced Lily. "It seems you're pretty popular in these parts."

"Because I'm your wife," Lily said.

"Maybe that hasn't hurt any, but I'd say you've won most of your fans on your own. Your talent and being a good parent and just generally being a decent sort."

"For an Easterner?"

"For an Easterner, nothing. Buck says a number of people told him you're more what Haiku Valley is about than he and Jack put together. They wondered if you would drop any legal action you were considering against them if they print a retraction in next week's *Herald*."

"I never was considering any legal action." Lily laughed. "But I don't suppose you told them that."

"I did, dammit. I told them the truth. That I'd taken

Jack's letter as seriously as a declaration of war, and you'd just smiled and gone about your business. I thought that would irritate Buck, but he looked relieved. He said he wanted the retraction to appear in print, anyway. Not out of a sense of justice, I don't think, as much as self-protection. I'm supposed to tell him your reaction."

"I'll tell him myself," Lily said. "If Jack wants to print a retraction, fine, as long as it also mentions the Venables' tasting room. More important, I want Jack and Muriel Clarkson and Buck and Sarah Olly in the audience tonight. Missy deserves to have her opening attended by her parents and her parents' closest friends."

"I thought you were all sold out," Tom said.

Lily shrugged. "If the White House called, we'd find four tickets, wouldn't we? Florence and I will work something out. Tom—"

"Lily—"

"I think it's my turn," she said.

"Wait. I haven't finished." He came over and sat down next to her. "I was just plain wrongheaded about that business with Jack. I think I was so thrown by Mark's coming that I lost all perspective."

Lily looked wonderingly at him. "You were thrown?"

"Well, you knew it all along," he said a trifle impatiently.

"Yes, but I didn't know you knew it. You kept saying it wasn't so."

"I had a moment of truth with myself after the meeting with Buck," Tom said. "Some of what you

said about my being too much of the man of iron—
well, it was true. I couldn't admit your airy approach
to Jack was right, and I couldn't admit I was jealous
of Mark, and it was all part of the same thing."

"Nobody likes to admit to dark emotions," Lily
said. "Until I saw Jack Clarkson I didn't know how
angry I was at him. And I think maybe my letting the
anger show was all to the good. He may want to do
battle again, you know, even if he writes a letter of
retraction. He's pretty passionate about his ideas. But
he'll think twice about doing anything behind my back.
I guess we both have a little more respect for each
other."

Tom put his arms around Lily. "Dearest—" he
began.

"No, let *me* finish." Lily breathed in the wonderful
spice of his chest as if it were a courage-giving ether.
"Sometimes tender emotions are hard to admit to,
also. I had to admit that I'd loved Mark in the past
to make the present be true and right. It seemed so
awful to acknowledge I'd loved any man other than
you, though. And to admit that love sometimes dies,
as if the admission would make our love more fragile."

"It isn't fragile," Tom said, making soothing motions in her hair. "It's the rock of the Western world.
Me not man of iron, but it love of iron."

"You dear, silly man. Most wonderful of men. I
didn't chip away at the rock with my awful comment
about you and Cleo? Tom, did you figure out what I
was really saying? That I was wishing you were her
only father and our life was simpler?"

"When I cooled down, I did put it together. But I

wouldn't want Cleo to be different. I wouldn't want anything to be different. I think you chose well in both her fathers."

"You mean it?" Lily raised her head to meet the warmth in his eyes.

"I do. I feel purged, somehow. I was jealous of Mark, and I came to terms with it, and now I find myself kind of liking him."

Lily's chest heaved with relief. The bad dream was over.

"If you're retiring as the man of iron," she said, "does that mean I get to take off my Wonder Woman costume now and then?"

"Absolutely," Tom said. His hands went to the buttons of her lavender dress. "Let's begin with now. Allow me?"

Her clothes, and then his, seemed to melt away from them. Wordlessly they glided toward their bed.

Their hands moved everywhere on each other's bodies, reclaiming, reaffirming. Their lips clung together, sealing the moment and promising the future. Limbs entwining unhurriedly, they felt themselves being drawn into total union. They didn't so much make love as let love make them.

Cresting with Tom, Lily felt bonded to him as never before. She knew that bad dreams might come again, but the dawn would always follow. They belonged together for the ages. Fear would never own her again.

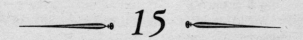

15

"BRAVA!" SHOUTED JACK CLARKSON as Missy Clarkson took her curtain calls. Next to him, Muriel wiped tears from her eyes.

"A star is born," Tom whispered to Lily.

"Maybe more than a star," Lily whispered back. "Look at those rapturous looks Mark is giving her."

"Maybe your admitting to having loved him freed him from you," Tom said.

"Do you suppose? It seems an unlikely match— but you never know. We'll just have to wait and see if she starts smelling of Night Blooming Lilies."

"Oh, how I love you, Lily Langdon."

"No more than I love you, my Tom."

Leading the well-satisfied crowd of theatergoers out toward dessert and coffee, Lily noticed Cleo, on her own.

"Where's Gideon, honey?" she asked.

"He said I was neglecting my father and it wasn't fair because Gideon would always be here but Mark would soon be back in New York."

"That's quite a young man," Lily said approvingly.

To her astonishment, Cleo made a cross face. "Please don't try to rush me into anything, Mother."

As Cleo went off in search of Mark, Lily turned to Tom with a sigh. "Will I ever totally understand the human heart?"

"Will anyone?"

"Would life be as exciting if we knew it all?" Lily countered.

Arm in arm, needing no words, they wandered out behind the theater, watching the moon hang bright and heavy over the vineyards, not a trace of cloud in the sky.

WONDERFUL ROMANCE NEWS!

Do you know about the exciting SECOND CHANCE AT LOVE/TO HAVE AND TO HOLD newsletter? Are you on our *free* mailing list? If reading all about your favorite authors, getting sneak previews of their latest releases, and being filled in on all the latest happenings and events in the romance world sounds good to you, then you'll love our SECOND CHANCE AT LOVE and TO HAVE AND TO HOLD Romance News.

If you'd like to be added to our mailing list, just fill out the coupon below and send it in...and we'll send you your *free* newsletter every three months — hot off the press.

☐ *Yes, I would like to receive your free SECOND CHANCE AT LOVE/TO HAVE AND TO HOLD newsletter.*

Name _____

Address _____

City _____ **State/Zip** _____

Please return this coupon to:

Berkley Publishing
200 Madison Avenue, New York, New York 10016
Att: Irene Majuk

HERE'S WHAT READERS
ARE SAYING ABOUT

To Have and to Hold™

"Your TO HAVE AND TO HOLD series is
a fabulous and long overdue idea."
— *A. D., Upper Darby, PA**

"I have been reading romance novels for over
ten years and feel the TO HAVE AND TO HOLD
series is the best I have read. It's exciting,
sensitive, refreshing, well written. Many thanks
for a series of books I can relate to."
— *O. K., Bensalem, PA**

"I enjoy your books tremendously."
— *J. C., Houston, TX**

"I love the books and read them over and over."
— *E. K., Warren, MI**

"You have another winner with the new TO HAVE
AND TO HOLD series."
— *R. P., Lincoln Park, MI**

"I love the new series TO HAVE AND TO HOLD."
— *M. L., Cleveland, OH**

"I've never written a fan letter before, but
TO HAVE AND TO HOLD is fantastic."
— *E. S., Narberth, PA**

*Name and address available upon request

Second Chance at Love.